Native
Love Jams

TASHIA HART

Real Native Romance

NOT TOO FAR REMOVED PRESS 2023

Acknowledgements

Chi-miigwech to everyone at the Native American Community Development Institute (NACDI) and the All My Relations Arts, Native Authors Program; to my fellow Native authors in the program; to Diane Wilson, a Dakota author and Native writing group mentor; to Mona Susan Power, a Dakota author who provided our group with constructive feedback; to the Northland Foundation for their support through a Maada'ookiing Grant; to everyone who supported the book through fundraising; to my community of friends and mentors who helped me fine tune things; and to my loves, my husband Jonathan and our son, Mino.

Prologue

The last man drinking, swivels suds at the bottom of his glass.

Where's that fucker that was talking to my girl? he thinks, glaring into the now dimly lit kitchen beyond the bar.

"Get ya anything before close, Chris?" the bartender asks the man.

One of the cooks exits the kitchen and tosses his jacket on an empty stool.

There you are.

"Got a light?" Chris asks the cook.

"Yeah," the cook says.

"Niigaanii," a co-worker calls the cook back to the kitchen.

"It's in my jacket pocket," Niigaanii says before disappearing through the double doors.

A few minutes later, Niigaanii exits the kitchen to find both Chris and his jacket gone.

***

Two blocks over, Chris stands wavering in front of a health food store. He pulls a lighter from the pocket of his new jacket and lights a cigarette.

He steadies himself with the help of a baseball bat, "None of you fuckers can have her," he says, slipping into the darkness of the store.

Winnow

Winnow weaves her roasted-hazelnut-brown hair into a messy side braid and grabs a gallon jar from a kitchen shelf. She turns it, gently tumbling the inhabitants. Several fist-sized, hard-as-rock pieces of birch fungus clink against the glass. The lid of the jar bears the scuffs, dents, and tape residue from a year in utility. The oldest mark, from when the jar was new and held the promise of a wild food enterprise, is worn but legible; an ink stamping that reads "Wild at Hart," Hart being a nod to her last name.

July morning sunshine scatters through the jar, creating a kaleidoscope effect on the walls and counter. The sparkle reminds her of the glittering, knee-cutting snow she trudged through to chop the fungus from the crook of an old tree last winter. It was twenty below with the wind howling, the sweet smell of the woody interior of the fungus called chaga, suppressed by the cold but still detectable. Her only companion, a trusty hatchet.

Despite losing sight of her dream when someone vandalized the commercial kitchen she worked in, she's built a life hiking through

rough terrain and swarms of insects to find, converse with, and harvest plants for food and medicine. Her latest gig to forage and cook for a wild food festival in northern Minnesota would be more exciting if she wasn't also packing to leave her home and fiancé behind.

Ex-fiancé, she thinks, trying the prefix out for the first time since receiving carnal images of her fiancé Chris and his coworker Emily in a group chat by mistake.

Winnow's cousin Melanie, a thirty-two-year-old, dark-haired woman in an all-black ensemble of sweatpants, an off-the-shoulder, short-sleeved sweatshirt, and beaded hoop earrings, sits on the floor nearby. She stretches her legs around an oversized box labeled "kitchen stuff" and sniffs a bag of dried ramps before tucking them inside. She picks up Winnow's phone from the floor and resumes reading, "I knew you love blondes best. Winky face emoji."

"Can you please stop reading that out loud?"

Melanie lays the phone back down on the floor. Her eyes squint to slits, enlarging her smoky shadowed lids, "Yuck, I hate Emily. I'm glad you're leaving Chris. He done messed up beyond all repair this time, Win."

The fact that Emily is Winnow's opposite stings the most. She looks down at her everyday self: cutoff jean shorts; loose, front tucked t-shirt with the fading image of a nerdy frog; and mismatched, slouchy socks. Not the kind made to slouch but slouchy because even though she can afford new ones, she grew up poor and learned how to get the most use out of a thing before repurposing, donating, or finally throwing it out.

Winnow's utilitarian outlook on life was an ongoing source of embarrassment for Chris. Like the time he picked her up after work to meet his coworkers and halfway through dinner she excused herself, announcing she found a wood tick in her sock. After his chiding, she swore to quietly let loose on him the next arachnid she found rather than flush it down the toilet. Which is exactly what she did. He found the tick at the nape of his neck after two days; by then, it was starting to swell and turn grey. Then there was the time, dried mud stained the rear of her jeans from digging cattail rhizomes. Or the time she had the option of calamine lotion or an oozing patch of poison ivy on her face. Or the bee sting between her eyes. Or the hundred other things.

In addition to looking the part of a woman who spends most of her time in the wilderness, Winnow gave up makeup decades ago and is now thirty-three and as Chris would say, "frumpy."

She wonders from time to time if there is anyone out there who would appreciate her unkempt eyebrows, undusted cheeks, and mink-free eyelashes.

Just let it go.

She does her best to relax her body. Her shoulders soften, she didn't know they were tense. Her eyebrows unfold, and her face lightens. Her stomach unwinds, and the accompanying noise makes her gasp in surprise.

Melanie pulls her shirt up over her face, and fans the air between them, "Jeez Win, what'd you eat?"

Nearby, junk food wrappers spill from the top of the trashcan like a heap of sad confetti. What hadn't she eaten? Normally, it's whole foods with dairy and sweets at a minimum. In her anguish, she consumed Chris' junk food stash. Making their way through her intestines are gas station sandwiches, candy bar-flavored ice cream, and an assortment of potato chips. It'll be days before her digestive system and sugar-sensitive skin clears up.

Good thing I don't have anyone to impress this week, she thinks. *It's not like I'm going to find the man of my dreams in a berry patch.*

Niigaanii

"Come on out of there Mr. Puppers and get yourself some breakfast," Niigaanii says to the scruffy patch of brindle fur and half-missing ear sticking around the side of the workshop. "I'll be leaving soon; I've got berries to pick on my way to the kitchen."

Mr. Puppers, also known as Dinky, Scruffy, and a dozen other names around the rez, tilts his head sideways, revealing an inquisitive eye to accompany the ear. He pauses, fur aglow; the pinkish-orange rays of the early morning sun kiss his face, causing him to squint.

Since his arrival two weeks ago, Mr. Puppers has made his bed not in the abandoned fox den, nor in the weatherized, multi-unit doghouse Niigaanii built for the strays, but under the brand-new food truck with four-wheel drive, all-terrain tires, and shiny chrome hubcaps Niigaanii keeps parked behind the shed.

The truck was acquired by the tribe a few months back, and Niigaanii being the Rainy Bay Community Center and Hotel kitchen manager, was tasked with putting it to use. The Harvester, he calls it, is now Rainy Bay Nation's first FSAV, Food Sovereignty in Action

Vehicle, a wild foods processing, and delivery vehicle. As soon as he finds a new kitchen manager, he'll work on The Harvester full-time.

After installing specialty sinks, coolers, storage racks, and later this week—a custom vinyl wrap—all The Harvester needs is a freeze dryer. That requires getting his boss, his sister Bibs, to approve his purchase order. In the meantime, he's still on the lookout to hire someone for the mobile food crew.

"You feel like oatmeal today?" Niigaanii asks Mr. Puppers. He brushes a mosquito from the front of his grey, sleeveless, hooded t-shirt, and wafts at another before it can probe a scar above his left eyebrow, "I don't have any bacon grease to go with that oatmeal."

Mr. Puppers snorts.

"I do have some leftover ogaa naboob though. That'll start us both off on the right track. You know what they say, the best part of waking up, is ogaa naboob in your makak." Niigaanii chuckles to himself.

Mr. Puppers takes a few steps forward, and sits down perkily, as if to say, "I'm ready."

"Alright, ogaa naboob it is."

Niigaanii fetches an oversized, red ceramic soup mug with a broken handle and a white letter N sitting on the ground near the shed. A matching one with the letter C lays nearby accumulating pill bugs. Remnants of his last relationship, the dishes have avoided the wastebin despite their degree of disrepair.

He gives it a rub on his light-wash denim jeans and goes to his cabin to fill it with soup. He puts the mug down in front of the dog, who begins his approach, and then stops; his bright, amber eyes watching intelligently.

The dog licks his lips and dances his front paws on the ground with excitement.

Niigaanii backs up to give the pup room to eat comfortably and walks back to the porch. He picks up his own dish, a glass pint jar, and sits down on the steps to eat.

"We have a visitor coming this week," he says between bites, "a cook."

The dog makes eye contact while maintaining a steady lap.

Niigaanii chuckles, "I don't know, she might be as good of a cook as me, but this is a family recipe," he motions to his walleye soup, "so she probably doesn't make her ogaa naboob how you're accustomed to, but it might be just as good."

Satisfied with the conversation, Mr. Puppers returns his gaze to his breakfast.

After they finish eating, Niigaanii collects the licked-clean soup mug, "We're looking for a dishwasher for the community center, you interested?"

Mr. Puppers scratches his underbelly with a back leg, stretches his neck out, and flattens his ears against his head in sweet repose then busies himself in the juniper bushes along the cabin where rabbits hang out.

Niigaanii cleans the dishes and fills his pint jar with coffee before jumping in his pickup, "You have a good day now, Mr. Puppers. Gigawaabamin zhebaa."

Winnow

"Just my knives left," Winnow says. She plucks her favorite santoku from a magnetic block and tucks the blade into her knife roll.

Her phone vibrates.

It's a text from Emily. *Hey, Winnow, good morning, did you get the pictures I sent last night? You haven't responded so I was wondering if they went through.*

Winnow's eyes narrow, "Is she serious?" Her thumbs fly to get out a reply. *I didn't get any pictures. Can you send them again? My phone has been acting up for weeks. Thx!*

It was true that her phone had been acting up, but not in this case.

She picks up her cleaver. *SLAM!* She hefts on it with both hands to get it unstuck from the wooden cutting board.

The next message is from Chris. *Morning babe! How was your night? Did you sleep well? I'm not sure what I did to my neck but it's killing me. Probably these hard-ass hotel pillows. I might take some*

Ibuprofen and skip the first session this morning and just chill in my room until I can move it. Love you.

"I know what you did! You god," *WHAM!* "damn," *SLAM!* "hoochie," *WHAM!* "coochie," *BAM!* "chomper!" she yells, pulling the cleaver out again and again.

She hurls the cutting board across the kitchen. It hits the crockpot, sending ceramic shards to the floor.

She speaks in a mocking tone as she types her reply to Chris, "Morning babe! I just woke up. Crashed out early last night. Sorry you're not feeling well. I'm gonna some make coffee and get organized for my trip later this week. Hope you feel better soon."

Winnow and Melanie stare at the phone. Alas, it lights up again.

It's Emily. *No biggie, it was just some cool architecture of the city.*

Winnow stomps across the room. She picks up a half-eaten bag of chips and heads down the hall to the bedroom. She pours the chips into Chris' pillow and smashes around the room with it. When she tires, she returns to the kitchen.

Melanie raises an eyebrow.

Winnow shrugs.

Still craving revenge, Winnow jumps on the next idea that pops into her head. She scrolls back in her messages to a conversation with a chef friend who has a thing for her.

She types feverishly. *Has the position been filled?*

Niigaanii

N iigaanii sips coffee from his jar and cruises dirt roads winding through maples, birch, and pine. He stops to pay special attention to the fruiting plants, hanging his head out the window in the cool, dewy morning air. The nape of his neck dampens, producing chills. He lets loose his shoulder-blade-length ponytail of dark, wavy locks to cover it.

The last sip of makade-mashkikiwaaboo twinkles in the sunlight, the caramel liquid lapping the bottom of the vessel. A vessel whose original contents serendipitously led him to leave his job in Minneapolis a year ago and return home. A vessel that despite Cindy walking out on him, helped him maintain his vision. A vessel that still has a blue "Wild at Hart" stamp on the lid to match the blueberry jam the jar held.

He finishes his coffee and stops at the Trading Post down the road from the Rainy Bay Community Center and Hotel, a building complex where most of the reservation's activities are held. In the parking lot, he runs into his older cousin, Jay.

"Aaniin, niij," Jay says.

"Aaniin."

"Hey, guess what? I'm starting a business."

Niigaanii chuckles, remembering the last time he saw his cousin.

Jay helped for a day on The Harvester as a trial for the mobile food crew position a month back. They spent the morning with their noses to the forest floor, watching for the bright-orange pop of chanterelles. After gathering a cooler full of the delectable-when-cooked fungi, they parked at the Trading Post to sort the mushrooms before distributing them to the community kitchens around the rez.

Niigaanii left Jay in charge of getting the mushrooms portioned and packed into the cooler on The Harvester while he helped the under-staffed Trading Post deli crew with their lunch rush. Jay left the back door of the truck open while he played pinner poker—poker for pinners of weed—at the truck's service window with a couple of guys from town. Someone walked off with the mushrooms and Jay walked home less a job but with a few more pinners than he had at the start of the day.

"What scheme you got going this time?" Niigaanii says.

"A carwash. I'm using the old community center parking lot on weekends to get it going. I'm calling it, NeeJee's SqueeJees." He holds his hands up to frame the air as if imagining the name in lights, "Whaddya think?"

"I'll be the first in line," Niigaanii says, motioning to the fresh mud on his truck from the morning's drive.

Jay smooths his black mustache that's nearly long enough to cover his missing front tooth, "You get that freeze dryer yet?"

"Gaawiin, but all I gotta do is take the cook Bibs hired out foraging this week and she'll sign off on it." He smiles, "It'll be a piece of wiishkobi-bakwezhigan."

Jay laughs, "Whatever you say, niij." He hits Niigaanii on the side of the arm with his newspaper, tucks the back of his blue tank top into the black leather belt holding up his jeans, and hops into his 1989 town car. He slides his caramel aviators on, cranks up the powwow tunes, and kicks up pebbles on his way out of the parking lot.

Niigaanii chuckles, "Nice car," he says regarding Jay's new wheels.

Inside the Trading Post, an older man is standing behind the counter looking captivated by his cell phone. He doesn't look up when Niigaanii enters.

Niigaanii grabs a bottle of locally made iced tea from a cooler. He sets it on the counter along with a newspaper, "Morning Merle. This batch any good?"

Merle continues to peer over the top of his glasses, still absorbed in his phone, "It'd be better if you'd get out to the big island for some miinan. We've used the frozen ones up."

Merle and his wife Marissa started making wild fruit teas a few summers back and rely on local harvesters for their ingredients. The summer Cindy left, last summer, was the last time Niigaanii brought a harvest of blueberries back from the island. He did it for years, bringing wild fruits and fish to share with the community, minus the year he spent in the Twin Cities while Cindy pursued her dream of being a blues singer.

"There's good patches of berries closer than the island," Niigaanii says.

Merle offers him an unamused look in response to this statement.

Niigaanii ignores it and continues, "Juneberries are ripe behind the powwow grounds, blueberries along the old south forest road are plumping up, chokecherries on Potato Hill won't be ripe for a while."

While all good locations, these patches of fruit are nothing compared to the motherload on the big island, one of two in Rainy Bay's main lake. But Merle doesn't need to tell Niigaanii this. He knows.

Merle sweeps a stray bit of gray and black hair behind his left ear, causing his bright-green, paisley bandana to hike up on that side.

"Four-fifty," Merle says, regarding the bottle of tea and newspaper, "Oh!" He slides a mostly blank, maroon pocketbook across the counter, "Write your number down, eh? Lost my address book again."

Niigaanii grabs a pen from the can, "You know you can put this on your phone now, right?"

"Don't trust 'em," Merle says, reading his phone.

Niigaanii scrawls his information down, "I hear ya." He hasn't had a cell phone in years and prefers it that way.

Merle adjusts his bandana over his ear, "What's the name of that cook who's coming this week? I'm looking her up on my social media."

Niigaanii's relieved Merle isn't interested in further discussion of the island, or the reason Niigaanii hadn't been there in a year: Cindy turning down his marriage proposal on the island during their fifth-anniversary hiking trip.

Niigaanii puts the money on the counter, "I don't know. Bibs probably told me, but I forget."

Niigaanii was in fact, guilty of not remembering the names of several women since Cindy. Like Amanda, or as Niigaanii remembers her, the flycatcher. Amanda is Bibs' friend from bingo she brought over for dinner one night without telling him. All he remembers is her large, hair-sprayed bangs capturing a tiny fruit fly to her forehead the entire night. And there was Nila, Johanna, and Rebecca; or as Niigaanii recalls them: the arm puncher, high-chuckler, and spinach tooth. He couldn't help that his love for Cindy doomed him from making meaningful connections with other women. He had, however, thought less about Cindy the last few months.

"Oh! Here she is." Merle reads quietly for a moment then faces his phone towards Niigaanii, "Her name's Winnow. She's from Red Lake."

Winnow's profile picture is of two little strawberries whose combined stems take the shape of a green heart. Niigaanii nods his head, "Winnow H. She's cute," He says, regarding the strawberries, seeing how there are no pictures of Winnow H.'s actual likeness.

Merle continues to hold his phone for Niigaanii to peruse.

"You know I stay away from social media, Merle. She's supposed to be here on Wednesday. I'll get to meet the woman behind the strawberries then."

Merle smiles but remains persistent with his urging of Niigaanii to scroll through her profile.

Seeing Merle means business, Niigaanii obliges his friend and takes the phone.

"Oh, no," Niigaanii says.

"What do you mean, 'Oh no?' I find a wife for you, and this is what you do."

"This says she's engaged."

Merle throws his hands in the air as if to say, "So what?"

"Ah, Merle," Niigaanii shakes his head, "You remember the guy from the city that got me thrown in jail? The whole reason Cindy left?"

Merle listened to Niigaanii talk about the guy, Chris Brown, frequently in the months following Cindy's departure but keeps his comments about Cindy's departure to himself, "Yeah?" Merle says.

"That's who she's engaged to."

Winnow

"Can we finally laugh at how stupid Chris' taste in music is?" Melanie says, her darkly painted lips lifted in a crinkled purse. Her silky black hair, pinned up in a half-bun, bobs with sass as she tosses her head back and forth. She fixes the strap of her bra, situates her shirt, and picks up a cd from a large stack of what could be any number of terrible 2000s bands. "This stuff was barely forgivable when it came out," she says, and fakes barfing. She pulls a bobby pin from her hair, lifts the lid of the cd case, and scratches at it until she's satisfied. She closes the case and puts it back on the stack.

"It's really bad," Winnow says, a flicker of laughter fizzling out before it can erupt. Everything with Chris was chaos, and towards the end, there was always a lingering, ambient anxiety between them. Somewhere along the way, Winnow forgot how to laugh. "Our *relationship* was a bad song. One rotten riff after another," she says.

Melanie plays the last cd Chris had in the player and dances around in as wacky a manner as possible, "We gotta break the bad association.

This music sucks, but you don't have to remember Chris when you hear it. You can remember me."

Winnow smiles.

She's gorgeous.

Melanie has always been Winnow's standard of beauty. Called exotic by folks in the border towns nearest the reservation yet she could be anyone's sister, cousin, or auntie on the rez.

As Melanie dances, the crushing feeling of betrayal lifts, and the promise of the essential life nutrients of laughter and family, awakens muscle memory from her youth.

"I feel like I haven't laughed since we were kids."

Melanie turns the stereo off, "Aww, cuz. Pretty soon, you're not gonna remember what it's like not to laugh."

Winnow's pocket vibrates.

It's her chef friend, Jeff. *Winnow! I have just the position in mind for you! I'll beg... if it'll make you come.*

Queasiness stinks up her stomach.

She's not in love with Jeff, her chef friend that's opening a restaurant in Bemidji where she'll soon live, but what else is she going to do with her life now that it was burst wide open?

Melanie props her head on Winnow's shoulder, reading.

Winnow replies. *I'm looking forward to coming after my gig up north this week. I'll let you beg then.*

Jeff's reply is instant. *Really? YES, PLEASE!!! Let me know when you're on your way. I'll do whatever it takes to bring you on board.*

"Ugh, gross," Melanie says, "Seriously? That guy, Win? You know he's a perv-ball, right?"

"What does it matter if Jeff comes next? Every guy I meet thinks I'm some weirdo nut who talks to plants and can't find the inky end of an eyeliner."

"It matters. *You* matter." Melanie takes the phone, turns the notifications off, and gives it back, "Help him get his restaurant going, fine, but do you need extra emotional baggage right now? I know you're really mad, but come on, Win, not Jeff," she says his name in an icky voice.

"Maybe he can bang some emotional clarity into me."

"Ew, you're better than this. You gotta let Chris go. Or not, I mean the choice is yours, but either way, you need to let go of that crazy energy building inside you because it's only going to get you hurt. Trust me, I know," Melanie says, giving her a hug, "You deserve to be with someone who loves you the way you are. That includes your smelly feet, the juice mustache you've had since you were five, and backward pajamas," Melanie kisses Winnow on the cheek.

"I was five! What do you want from me? And how is it on me that you've always had a fascination with smelling people's feet?" Winnow says, pulling her arms into her shirt and swinging it around the right way. She takes slow, drawn-out strides to the couch and sits down in front of a laundry basket of Chris' clothes. She digs into the basket again and again.

"What are you doing?"

"Making busy work for Chris," she says, tying knots into everything, "You know what's interesting? With every sock I knotted, the feeling of being emotionally knotted up with Chris got a little looser."

"That's flipping beautiful, Win."

Winnow dumps the contents of the basket behind the couch, "You're right. I don't want to have anything to do with Chris ever again. I don't want to talk to him, I don't want to think about him, and I sure as hell don't want to see him or Emily. Fuck'em." She hands Melanie her phone, "Text him back for me. Tell him, 'Love you.'"

Melanie raises an eyebrow before typing as she's told.

"I don't want him to know I know anything. I want him to shit his pants until he comes home to an empty house and never sees or hears from me again. That's what he deserves. I can't keep forgiving him. I'm like, totally, finally, ready to do something—somebody—else with my life." She closes her eyes and juts her chin up in a cheesy smile.

Melanie shakes her head but can't help but laugh, "And I'm going to help you." She sends the message, "Want me to block his number?"

Winnow gives her a guilty look, "I'm not quite there yet."

"So, what's your plan for when he calls and texts?"

"I'll ignore it."

Melanie kisses Winnow on the cheek, sure in Winnow's ability to ignore Chris, "It's nine. Jonny will be here soon to help load your stuff in his van."

Winnow looks around, taking in the remainder of the life she's leaving behind; it feels like an empty hull. It strikes her that it has for some time.

"Thanks for coming to my rescue, Mel. All I want to do this week is hang out, go to Rainy Bay, go foraging, and forget about Chris."

Melanie shrugs, "Fuck it. Let's go to Rainy Bay early."

"What?"

"Yeah, after we load Jonny's truck with your shit, we'll drive up, check in early, and relax for a couple days before your gig starts. I hear they got a good swimming beach up there."

"What about your stuff for the trip?"

"My bag's in the car. I didn't know what was gonna go down when I got here."

"Who'll let Jonny into your place?"

"He has a key," she says.

"What the hell, let's stoodis. Let's go to Rainy Bay early."

18

Melanie smiles her widest smile, the one that pulls her top lip up like a theater curtain, showing the space between her front teeth that long ago marveled back-of-town rez kids because she could spit through it and hold coins in there, "Hell yeah, cuzzin, let's sko!"

Niigaanii

"I'm not taking this woman," Niigaanii looks at Merle's phone to check her name, "Winnow H. foraging and I'm not working in the kitchen with her either. Who marries a guy like Chris Brown? Whatever. I'll find some other way to help out for the festival."

Niigaanii turns away from the counter, but instead of following his initial urge to walk out, he leans his back on it and runs his fingers through his hair.

"Jeez, Merle. I haven't thought about her in a while. Cindy, that is. Dammit, I was looking forward to this week until now."

Niigaanii avoids exchanging looks with Merle. He knows how absurd it is to suggest his absence from the kitchen for the nation's first-ever food festival, "I don't know what I'll do if that asshole shows up here."

"Forget about Chris Brown. If you ask me, Cindy was looking for a reason to leave and used the Chris Brown incident as an excuse."

Despite rumors of infidelity on Cindy's part, Niigaanii chose to trust her as he knew her, something he wished she'd done for him.

20

Instead, she chose to think he vandalized the health food store in the Twin Cities a year back.

Niigaanii turns around, "I wasn't asking, Merle." He grabs the tea and newspaper and walks towards the door, "Naagaj," he says before leaving.

Just down the road from the Trading Post, Niigaanii arrives at the community center. He shuts the engine off near a maintenance building at the far end of the parking lot and watches as a man in camo basketball shorts, a white t-shirt, and black slide sandals with white socks, shakes a spray paint bottle. A stereo on one of the tables plays old-school hip-hop music and the man, who's facing away from Niigaanii, occasionally busts a move as he rummages through bins and selects colors.

"Merle, pfft, what does he know? Just bandannas and scratch-offs and," he takes a drink of the tea, "mmm." He holds up the bottle, "Strawberry Swamp."

The label describes it as a blend of what the local Anishinaabeg call mashkigobag or swamp tea, indicating the habitat in which the plant lives. The other ingredients are wild strawberries and maple sugar.

He takes another drink, "Damn it's hard to be mad at you, Merle."

He closes his eyes, remembering the frosty, start-of-the-year hike he made out to the frozen bog on the western side of the reservation to harvest the evergreen shrubs needed for this very batch of tea. It was a perfect day. Even in his mind's eye, the familiar silhouette of mashkigobag, like tiny pine trees cresting above the snow, excite him. He places his asemaa near one of the plants before picking a few leaves and turning them over in his palm; the pop of rust-orange fuzz clinging to the bottoms. He nuzzles a leaf against his cheek to feel the soft caress of their fuzz on his skin. He lifts the leaves in his palm to his nose and takes a breath, reviving in his senses the delicate, floral aroma of the plant along with decades of good memories associated with the smell. One of his favorite scents. He looks around the quiet, frozen bog. The black spruce trees are shaggy and still. The flash of spots in the corner of his eye tells him a downy woodpecker observes him.

Memory relived, he opens his eyes and looks down to his toes, wiggling in the moccasins Merle and Marissa gifted him in return for two large sacks of swamp tea.

Now in a much better mood, he unfolds the newspaper. An article detailing the upcoming food festival spans the front page. A picture of his sister Bibs and two women accompanies the article. Bibs holds a squash. Niigaanii studies her long hair. It's like their mother's and his own, the darkest brown with purple highlights in the sun. Her dark-frame glasses are lifted by her square cheeks. Niigaanii smiles. He too, inherited their father's square face. The caption reads, "Community center and hotel manager and Indigenous Food Days coordinator holds a squash grown by local master gardeners." The two women, the master gardeners, were caught mid-squabble.

The man turns around and sees him, "Jailbird!" He laughs and trots over to the side of the pickup, a bag of chips in hand.

It's Niigaanii's cousin, Bruce the "Little Moose" Moozoons. Bruce's brown, loose curls bounce around his shoulders but for the top half that's pulled into a ponytail.

"Come on man, 'jailbird'? We talked about this," Niigaanii says, putting down the paper. "How about I tell everyone about your fake teeth?"

"What the fuck, man?" Moozoons says, looking around, "That's fucked up. I tell you what, Niij. You find a girl you like, and you can tell her whatever you want about my winning smile." He pops a chip into his mouth and shows his wide, white, full sparkling smile dappled by bits of chips.

Moozoons offers the bag to Niigaanii.

"I don't need a girl. I've been fine, I'll be fine," Niigaanii says, looking into the bag that holds but a shake of crumbs.

"You alone, cuz. Whether you've been fine or not," Moozoons dumps the crumbs into his mouth and then turns to shoot the wrapper at the garbage can about ten paces away and misses, "is debatable." He trots to pick the wrapper up, sinks a closer shot, and hoofs his way back to the truck, wiping chip grease on his shirt.

"Don't you have a mural to paint?"

Moozoons turns away from the truck to show the side of the building he'll paint, "You know it." He looks back to Niigaanii, who drinks his tea with his eyes shut, "Krehh, put away those luscious lappers and give me a hand then."

Tea sprays everywhere, shooting into the bottle and over the back of Niigaanii's hand as he laughs. He pulls up his shirt, revealing a silver and turquoise belt buckle nestled beneath the red band of his jersey-knit boxer shorts. He wipes his mouth, "You wish you had smoochers like these."

"Shit, gichi-manidoo wouldn't allow it. I'd be too deadleh."

Niigaanii laughs, "Alright cuz, I'll let you get on with your deadly self. I gotta go see Bibs."

"I hear Raquel's scheming with Delores to get a date with you."

Niigaanii cups his hand to his ear and says, "What's that, Bibs? I'll be right there."

He starts the truck and hands the bottle of backwash tea to Moozoons.

Niigaanii backs his truck up.

"Can't run forever, cuz," Moozoons says and looks down at the bottle, remembers what's in it, and shoots it out at arm's length.

Niigaanii flips him the bird as he pulls away, "Watch me."

Bruce hollers, "Stop by later?"

"Might as well, since I'm so desperate for company!"

***

Walking into the community center, Niigaanii greets Bob "Old Dusty" sitting at his desk just inside the lobby doors. A veteran of about eighty-five years young, with grey hair, and a wiry frame, and holding the position of lead security guard since the building's construction in the early nineties.

Niigaanii nods, "Aaniin."

The old man nods his head in return.

Niigaanii hands him the newspaper he got from Merle.

Dusty smiles.

Niigaanii picks up the man's empty coffee cup from his desk, the same one Dusty's used the last twenty years. He marvels at how it's held up; just one small crack at the top, the rest of the cup holding its integrity. Niigaanii occasionally jokes with Dusty that his cup is held together by powerful medicine. The strong makade-mashkikiwaaboo Delores makes every morning. He walks over to the coffee airpot on the counter nearby and fills up the cup halfway and replenishes his own jar. He puts the mug down on Dusty's desk. Seeing the elder has his sight on the crossword, Niigaanii sets off towards the kitchen.

***

"You're looking sunny today," Niigaanii says, arriving in the kitchen to find Delores, the head cook and a tribal elder, flitting about merrily.

24

He leans on a stainless-steel counter near the ovens and waits for what's coming.

"You gotta give that Raquel a chance! She's a good girl," Delores blurts out as she bends into the oven to fetch a pan of corn muffins. She slides it onto a cooling rack and furrows her brow at him.

"Nice girl, huh? This doesn't have anything to do with a nice quilt, does it?"

She flaps his arm with an oven mitt, "Oh, pfft!" She shoots him a tricky little look. Her short, greying brown hair, fresh out of curlers, bounces perkily as she works pouring batter into tins. She smiles at him now, knowing she's busted, "Doesn't hurt that she's an excellent quilt-maker, piling them up in her room from what I hear."

Niigaanii chuckles. He's heard Delores talk about wanting a quilt to enjoy the three seasons porch her husband built her this spring. Just so happens, Raquel also heard her mention this and came up with a plan to contract Delores to get her a date with Niigaanii in exchange for one.

"She *is* a girl, that's part of the problem."

"She's twenty-two"

"She's a baby. Even if in some universe I could get over the age difference, I went to high school with her mother for Christ's sake, who's still the chairwoman, unless you forgot."

Delores looks unfazed, "I had three kids by the time I was twenty-two."

He grabs a corn muffin from the tin, knowing the only reason he's not being slapped with her mitt again is that he's got a leg up, "Have you thought any more about the kitchen manager position? Comes with a raise, you know."

"I'm not good with the computer and ordering ingredients and stuff."

"I thought I was a lost cause when I was training in. If I can learn, you can too."

"I thought you were a lost cause too," she says, elbowing him. "I don't know. I just like making my muffins and cooking for people. Been doing it twenty years."

"That's why you're perfect for the job. You know everything around here. A computer is just a tool; you're the one with the knowledge."

"A raise does sound nice," she changes the subject, "My muffins would be a lot better with miinan. Are you going out to the island this year or what?"

"Told Bibs I would. Merle needs blueberries too. We'll see. Maybe I'll go this week, make myself scarce while our guest chef takes over the kitchen." He pauses, realizing now is his chance to try and wedge space between Winnow and himself, "Tell you what, if you help me fill my prep shifts, I'll go out to the island *and* I'll take Raquel out this morning."

He smiles. Going to the island is sounding better by the minute. He pulls the muffin apart and shakes it to avoid the scorch of billowing steam.

Delores' face lights up, and she slaps him on the arm again, causing him to drop his bite, "Oh, you good boy!" She digs her phone out of her apron, pulls her red frame readers down from her curls, and types at a quickened pace to Raquel, who's been on standby since seven-thirty am.

"Have her meet me out front at nine," he grins, "and tell her to bring some work gloves. I'm taking her out to look for roadkill."

Winnow

The buildings and busy streets of the Twin Cities opened to off-ramps and fields miles back. The thick trees of central Minnesota are now whizzing by. Small lakes pop from around almost every bend, each one a miniature, picturesque paradise. Herons balance atop long legs as they stretch and peck in the shallows, blending in with the lazy sway of cattail leaves while beavers pile sticks on lodges.

Winnow presses her face to the glass as they pass three small, furry bodies on the side of the road, "Are you fucking kidding me? Why don't people slow the fuck down? Is it so hard to take two seconds out of your day? You kill a family of otters because what? You have to shit?"

"Aww man, there's a zhigaag," Melanie says as they pass a dead skunk lying next to a sign that reads Rainy Bay twelve miles. "Good thing you called ahead, I dunno where we'd stay if they were full tonight."

"Yeah," Winnow says, tucking away her cell, "Bibs, the one that hired me, offered me work on their foraging truck until the festival prep starts. I guess it's part of a new department and they don't have a crew yet. An FSAV, she called it, Food Sovereignty in Action Vehicle. A foraging food truck. Now that's exactly the kind of awesome I wanna do with my life right now."

"Awh, not Jeff?" Melanie says.

"Shut up."

"You do whatever makes you happy; I'll be chillin' on the beach. You have a menu for the dinner on Friday?"

"Loosely. It'll depend on what we can harvest and what the community brings to the kitchen to share."

"I remember the last time I helped, there were a bunch of geese, partridges, and those little... root balls."

"Wild potatoes?"

"Yeah, that's them! That event was wild."

"Wet and wild, in your case, if I remember right. Didn't you get caught masturbating in the hotel hallway?

"I wasn't in the hall, sheesh!" Melanie returns her eyes to the road and says quietly, "It was the ice room." She says it matter-of-factly as if it wasn't the first time she got caught masturbating in public. "That reminds me, I brought you something, in celebration of being single."

Winnow looks in the backseat but sees no clue, "What is it?"

"Let's just say, a little self-love always makes me feel better, and I think the same would apply to you."

"Uhm."

"You'll see. It can wait till we get home next week, though. You don't need to be distracted on the job. Hey, does anyone say gaped anymore?"

Winnow snaps her head at her cousin, "What?"

"I wish gaped would make a comeback. I used to hear it a few times, on a good week."

"I still hear it on occasion," Winnow's laugh returns, "Usually when you're around."

Melanie flows to the next topic, "Remember when I was dating Zhoon?"

Winnow rolls her eyes, "Ugh."

"I know, jeez, gimme a break, I was hungry in my twenties."

"When have you not been hungry?"

"It's not my fault there's so little to eat." Melanie hasn't dated much while waiting for her best friend Jonny to return her love. "Anyway," she snaps her eyes, "we went to a powwow up in Bois Forte together, and Zhoon ditched me to go buy weed. Fucker never came back. Had to call my auntie to pick me up."

"Deb?"

"Eya'. After Zhoon took off, I was waiting around and I met a guy from Rainy Bay."

Winnow ups an eyebrow, "Rainy Bay, you say?"

"I'm pretty sure I told you about him. This was like ten years ago though."

'Uhm?"

"He was the coolest guy I've ever met. Besides Jonny, of course. So sweet and fricken cute too! He said he loved blueberries, and you'd just given me a jar of jam to give to Gramma the last time I saw you."

Winnow gasps, "You liked him enough to disappoint Gramma?"

Melanie throws her head back in laughter, then holds her hand over her nose, "Shut up! Oh my god, I just remembered! The next morning, he texted me saying how good your jam was, even asked if he could have your number, aaaaye!" Melanie laughs.

"What!"

"But don't think he was trying to get at you. Because he wanted to cuddle with *me*."

Winnow's laughter flows in with more ease. It's followed by a few minutes of silence as they watch the green fly by. Pops of yellow lady slippers and the distinct whitish green of wild sage adorn the ditches. Winnow drops pins in the map on her phone for where things are growing in case the medicine is needed later. Her map is filled with enough pins that in certain parts of the state, she must zoom in to distinguish one location from another. Rainy Bay, which is north of the Twin Cities and east of Red Lake, however, has no such pins, and the idea of getting to explore the place excites her.

"So, who was he?"

"All I remember is he told me to call him Little Moose."

"Oh yeah! Didn't you lose your phone along with his number before you could call him?"

The pain on Melanie's face is real, "Man, Win, that shit's still not funny."

"How come you never went looking for him?"

Melanie laughs, "Jeez, I'm not a stalker."

"But he was good enough to get Gramma's jam."

"Shut up!"

A few minutes pass before Melanie speaks up, "We're going to find you a good one, one of these days, Win."

Winnow pulls her legs up to rest on the dash, getting comfy, "I could stand to meet a quality man."

"What qualities?"

Winnow rightens abruptly in her seat and leans forward, squinting through the bug splatter the limp wiper failed to clear.

They slow down to avoid hitting an eighties model light blue pick-up truck parked halfway on the shoulder facing the wrong direction on Winnow's side of the road.

30

They creep by the truck and Winnow flattens the tip of her nose on the window. A tingly sensation spreads like wildfire through her nether regions and her abdominals tighten with desire. She moves away from the window, her back firmly on the seat, "How about a thirty-something Native dude in a sleeveless, hooded t-shirt, light wash denim jeans, dark brown, wavy hair landing just below his shoulders," she says, describing the man who emerges from the ditch holding a shovel. He smiles at her and gives a small wave as they pass, "and the best, dimpled smile."

Melanie misses him, "That's specific. Phew," she says as the car fills with the aroma of a skunk.

Winnow pivots to keep an eye on the man.

After they pass, he trots to the other side of the road and scoops up what looks to be the source of the smell, his biceps bulging as he does so.

Winnow bounces in her seat, and a tortured squeak escapes her lips, emanating from somewhere down deep, "Pull over," she says.

"Why?"

"Just pull over."

Melanie pulls the car into the shoulder, "What's gotten into you?" She investigates the rearview mirror. The man is bending over the open gate of the truck, his backside towards them. She raises an eyebrow, "I think I know what you *want* getting into you. Or should I say, who?"

This isn't normal. What am I doing?

Winnow reprimands herself as she exits the vehicle, shutting the door in response to Melanie's question. Then again, what's normal? Now that she's single, the freedom to explore, including finding out who this man is, moves her forward. Her heart skips in the back of her throat as she checks for traffic, and nearly skips down the road.

The smell of skunk clings to her skin as she approaches him from behind.

He adjusts a piece of cardboard in the truck bed with one hand, holding the shovel with the dead critter in the other.

Winnow stumbles over what she should say, when a young woman with jaw-length blonde hair, a short, baby-pink, stretchy skirt, and a white, low-cut V-neck tank barely holding her bosom in, emerges from the ditch side of the truck.

"Throw it away!" she storms.

Winnow takes pause a few yards from the truck.

Is that... Emily?

Had she seen a woman, she wouldn't have told Melanie to pull over. She wouldn't have gotten out of the car. And she wouldn't be standing here now like a damn fool.

"It's not garbage," he says, cheerily.

Winnow's blood pumps hard, giving her tunnel vision. The sway of the young woman's hips is different than Emily's and looking at her face, Winnow sees she's a Native woman. Emily's not Native and walks holding her arms up like a rabbit sitting on its haunches.

Could she be his daughter? He looks too young to be her dad.

The young woman shares enough similarities with Emily, however, that Winnow's stomach wrenches in betrayal as if it were.

The woman makes horking noises and returns to the cab of the truck, slamming the door. She contorts in horror when she realizes the man's putting the skunk in the back. She jumps out, holding her nose, "I'm not riding with that thing back there stinking everything up!" She says in a nasally voice, pointing at the skunk accusingly.

"Then don't." He lays the shovel down next to the box with the skunk and takes off his gloves.

The woman snatches her purse out of the truck and storms up the highway in a lopsided gait, kicking up pebbles with a tall wedge sandal on one foot, the other one bare and crusty-bottomed like it recently squished in mud. She passes Winnow, her lips pursed, eyes narrow slits. She swings her arms angrily and curses her way toward Melanie's car and Rainy Bay.

"You need a ride?" Melanie asks her as she walks by.

The woman looks up and down the road, "Yeah, I need a ride." She shoots the man a last evil look. It's enough to make Melanie flinch and pull her head back into the car.

Before stomping around to the passenger door, the young woman pulls her sandal free and chucks it as hard as she can toward the man. It lands flat in the middle of the road about ten feet from Winnow. The woman takes Winnow's seat in the shotgun and slams the door.

Winnow gives Melanie a what-the-fuck look.

Melanie shrugs.

It's too late to slink back to the car undetected. He's looking right at her.

Winnow says of the skunk, "What are you gonna do with'em?"

His smile pulls to one side, causing a dimple on his chin to stand out, "Besides run-off women?" He chuckles, looking satisfied with himself and making Winnow believe it isn't the first time he's done this.

"Looks like *we'll* be taking your date home."

He motions to the skunk, "That's okay, this zhigaag is better riding company anyway."

So she was his date. But he'd rather ride with a skunk.

Winnow looks to where the young woman is downloading her grief onto Melanie.

"I see that."

He rubs his hands on his pants and holds one out, "I'm Niigaanii. Can I help you with something or did you come over here to tease me and make me sweat?"

Help me with something? Make you sweat?

She bites her lip and takes his hand, paying the skunk factor no mind. She grew up touching fish guts, with a fisherman for a father. His hand is warm and soft on the top side, and a little rough on the bottom.

There's something familiar about him.

"I saw the skunk and thought you might need some help." She looks to where the critter is tucked under a tarp, "But I see you have it covered."

He smiles and releases her hand.

Winnow tries to keep it casual, "My cousin heard there's a good swimming beach here. That's where we're headed."

"Your cousin heard right," he says, climbing into the truck and shutting the door, "Well, you have a good one, stranger."

Walking back to the car, she realizes she didn't introduce herself.

Stranger.

Winnow stares smiling out the window the rest of the way to Rainy Bay while the young woman, Raquel, tells them how she was set up with Niigaanii by a mutual friend.

"I got all dressed up to go out for breakfast and he wanted to feed me a skunk!"

Winnow suppresses a snicker.

Be nice. Just because she reminds you of Emily, doesn't mean you should treat her how you'd like to treat Emily, that, that...

"Where yous from anyway?" Raquel asks, breaking Winnow from her downward spiral.

"Red Lake," Melanie says, "Winnow's cooking for the festival in Rainy Bay this week."

"You're a cook? So is that hot asshole back there," she says, throwing her head to the highway behind them.

This catches Winnow's attention, "He is?" ˙

"Yeah, but good luck trying to get on that. I thought it'd be easy, seeing how everyone says he's the loneliest bastard in town."

This time it's Melanie who snickers.

"No wonder he tried to feed you a skunk," Winnow mumbles.

"What?" Raquel didn't hear the last part.

Winnow points her lips to Raquel's forehead, which she can see in the visor mirror, "I have a salve for those bites if you want some," she says and digs into the "essentials" pocket of her backpack that contains burn ointment, bug bite salve, and snack bars.

"Hey, miigwech," Raquel says. She takes the salve and continues on her rant, "Mr. Nice Guy took me down a trail buzzing so loud with mosquitos I couldn't hear myself think," she sticks a finger in her ear and wiggles it, as if to get the rest of the buzzing out, "I got bit on my," *fweet! fweet!* she whistles, indicating her you-know-what, "when my skirt was up." She lifts in her seat and applies salve to her behind. She offers the tin back to Winnow.

"You keep it," Winnow says.

Why was her skirt hiked up? Is it possible he doesn't like her but still did the deed with her?

"We're here!" Melanie exclaims.

Winnow's thankful to see the turn for the hotel to come into view. A trading post with a gas pump sits on the corner and they pull in.

I'm glad I'll have work to keep me busy this week. I don't have time to puzzle over men and their urges, ugh.

Melanie sees Winnow's long face, "What's the matter?" she asks after Raquel exits the car.

Winnow omits feeling jealous of a twenty-something woman because she shares similarities to Emily, "I wish I didn't have to show up here feeling like a fool."

"Chris is the fool. Any guy worth a damn would know how awesome you are after one day, one minute with you, Win."

Niigaanii

"I met a woman," Niigaanii says, surprising himself. He hasn't felt a spark for anyone since Cindy until the nosy woman on the road.

His sister Bibs, who's been staring quietly into the computer in her office since he walked in five minutes earlier, bobs her head around the screen, "What? Who?"

"When I was out with Raquel." His cheeks redden under his natural tan, and he smiles big, "She gave Raquel a ride back to town."

"Who's the woman? She from around here?"

"Dunno, can't say."

Bibs cocks an eyebrow as if being tested.

Knowing his statement was a teaser and not being able to stop himself, he adds, "There's something familiar about her... and she's gorgeous."

"Oh?"

He can't help feeding her more, it's not like he's ever going to see the woman again, "Like a rose bush that lives on the beach, rustling in sandy wind and sun all day." He trails off; she did say she was going to spend time at the beach in Rainy Bay. Maybe he *would* see her.

"Did you retrieve the zhigaag?"

"Yep," Niigaanii says, sitting down in a chair facing Bibs' desk, "Miigwech for the tip, I think it bought me some time off from ole grabby hands, Raquel."

"I mentioned the zhiigaag so you could fetch it for Olivia to make mashkiki. It wasn't salvageable?"

Niigaanii shakes his head, "Gaawiin."

Bibs returns her attention to the screen, "Those two young guys who helped deliver vegetables last weekend signed up for truck duty this week."

"Those two only signed up because they think Raquel's coming."

"Is she?"

"Not if I can help it."

"Then why do they think she is?"

"Because I told them she was so they would help out," he grins, "Despite being a couple of knuckleheads, they were a real help. They showed up on time and worked hard."

Bibs laughs, "Knuckleheads, huh? Sounds like someone else I knew when he was young."

"I think the older one, Derek, might be a good fit to work full-time on the truck. He's been trying to figure out what line of work to get into since he graduated a couple of years ago. He could use the cash to get some wheels. The younger one, Michael, works well with Delores. I might ask him if he wants the dishwasher job."

"That's good. Oh! That reminds me, I found another person to help on the truck."

"Who's that?"

"The woman who's coming to cook for the festival."

"What? She's coming on Wednesday, right?"

"She called a bit ago; she'll be here today."

She's not coming on The Harvester.

"What do you know about her?"

"I've never met her. I heard she's one of the chefs who cooks for these types of events."

"Did you know she's engaged to Chris Brown?"

"Chris Brown? The guy who got you arrested. Fuckin aye, I remember that shithead. He better not show his sorry ass around here or I'll put a boot to it." She kicks out from her desk and then drops her leg and laughs, rubbing her knee.

"Easy Sis. I see you're using the cane today."

"Mmhmm."

"How come?"

Bibs grabs her cane and hobbles back and forth by her desk, "Jeez my foot fell asleep. Carole needed help hauling a load of compost to the East Garden yesterday. I'm only a little sore today but I don't want it to get any worse before my date with Harvey tonight," she says.

He ignores the part about her date. He's not worried about Harvey, in maintenance. Harvey's a good guy. But the fact she's using her cane means she's in more pain than she's letting on.

"You were suppose'ta lemme know when that compost haul was gonna be."

"You can't be everywhere, brother, as much as you like to think you ken be. Find yourself a woman and you'll be less concerned with everyone else's problems.

"Am I dreaming to think there's someone out there who likes shoveling compost, having funerals for skunks, and spending as much time in the bush as me?"

Bibs eases into a bend and rummages through a box. She pulls out a t-shirt in his size and throws it to him, in exchange for the skunky one, which she tucks into a bag.

Niigaanii holds up the new green tee, "Always after the free exposure, this guy." He pulls it on, the word "Moozoons" stylized to look spray-painted on in magenta and neon yellow.

He reaches for the bag containing the skunky shirt, saying, "I can take that down to the laundry room."

She swings it out of his reach, "I got it," she smiles.

"Harvey must be working today, eh?" He chuckles. Maintenance is across from the laundry room. "Hey, about that chef that's coming. I think it makes more sense for her to be in the kitchen while I take the boys out to harvest this week. You know, cover our bases."

"She's a forager and wants to help gather, and that's what this event is about, sharing knowledge, experiences. We've got a lot of people signed up for cooking duty. Besides, Merle says she's very friendly; he recommended her for the job."

"Merle? He didn't tell me he met her. That's beside the point. What if her fiancé, Chris Brown is along? There's no way in hell he's coming on The Harvester."

"How do you know that's her fiancé anyway?"

"Merle's friends with her on social media."

"I wonder if she knows what he did."

"You see my problem? Either she's an asshole or I have to make sure I don't accidentally tell her. Wait, that could be the perfect revenge. I tell Chris Brown's fiancé what he did and she leaves him the way Cindy left me when she thought I did it."

Bibs sighs, "I tell you what. If she's alone, take her out and show her a good time. If Chris is along, I'll tell him there isn't enough seating on the truck. Please, do this for me. I want this event to be perfect, and we don't want our invited guests to feel unwelcome here. You do this and I'll sign the purchase orders for the rest of The Harvester's installs."

I don't want her and her shitty Chris Brown vibes anywhere near The Harvester. I'll find something else for her to do. Bibs won't know, she'll be busy with the rest of the festival.

Niigaanii knows Bibs' friendly ask is a decision. She is his boss, after all. He makes his way out of the office, "I'd rather not spend any time with the cook you hired, but I'll take her foraging if you sign that purchase order as soon as she leaves." He turns to see the woman from the road approaching the check-in counter.

It's her.

"Would you help our guest?" Bibs says and heads down the hall to maintenance.

"Hi," the woman says, "I'm Winnow. I'm the cook for the event this week."

Oh, shit.

Winnow

Winnow beams with excitement as they cruise along the canopy of sugar maples lining the dirt road to the Rainy Bay Community Center and Hotel. She hangs her head from the window and inhales as deeply as she's allowed with the wind rushing to get up her nose. Cool air released from the leaves of trees swaying in a gentle breeze mingles with aromas of wet moss and an understory full of greenery; a plethora of wild foods. In the shady parts, there are thimbleberries, hazelnut bushes habituating both shade and sun patches, and a few sun-loving fruit bushes as well as a variety of wild greens.

Knowing this week is about forging and fortifying relationships with humans and plant relatives, the world seems fuller, brighter, and overflowing with a palpable love that calms unmet desires of the flesh; the beauty in the world fills her up like a lover she never had but always hoped for.

They pull up to the hotel portico and stop behind a luxury vehicle with a blue parking placard on the rearview mirror. Melanie motions with her darkly painted lips to the entrance, "Can you grab us a cart? I gotta call my mom back."

Winnow hops out of Melanie's two-door her uncle gave her for helping him with three summers of moccasin-making across the Midwest. Melanie went to college for jewelry making and dropped out the first year when she was selling faster than she could supply. The trunk of the car is packed with beads, fabric, birchbark, and metal jewelry-making supplies. She'll leave the sorting of the bags for Melanie.

A bright-banana-yellow scooter is parked near the door and Winnow admires it on her way to the entry, which is empty of carts.

She hops back in with Melanie.

"I talked to my mom. They took my Auntie Deb to Bemidji in an ambulance. They're flying her to Duluth."

Winnow knows what this means. Melanie is leaving. Instead of begging her to stay, Winnow hugs her cousin around the neck and says, "I'm sorry about your auntie. I know you two are close." Melanie's aunt Deb has had health issues the last few years resulting in hospital stays and a couple of close calls.

"You gonna stay?" Melanie adds quickly, "You can come with me; we can go find a room in Duluth before Mom, Dad, and Weston arrive." Weston is Melanie's twelve-year-old nephew who lives with her parents.

Winnow looks to the trees, the smell of lake water pools in her nose causing her nose hairs to tingle with buoyancy. There's a familiarity to this place that shifts her emotional wobbliness towards the steady. And she doesn't want to leave before her job's done.

"I think I'm okay with staying."

Never mind my backup plan of calling Jeff to come and get me if I need to bail.

"Really? That's great! I mean, I'd love for you to come but I'm glad you're okay being here, alone." She grabs Winnow's arm, "Maybe you'll see that cute guy from the road," she says, as Winnow hops out of the car.

Just through the entryway, a security guard sits at a desk. He's got the crossword puzzle half done; the local newspaper is one she's never seen before, the Rainy Bay Babaamaajimo.

Dusty, his badge indicates, nods hello.

"The crossword any good today?" Winnow asks him.

He pooches his lips. The point lands on his empty coffee mug.

"It's hard to finish without coffee, eh? You need a refill?"

He smiles and nudges his cup with a left hand that looks like it's seen hard work and sunshine over the years; his four fingers straightened towards his palm with arthritis.

She picks up his mug and, following her nose to the smell of fresh-brewed coffee, finds two full airpots on a counter just beyond his desk. There's a closed, food tray window with music and voices inside. She pours Dusty a cup of regular. On her way back, she notices a door to a conference hall.

"Is that where the dinner's gonna be on Friday?" she asks Dusty, placing his mug down.

Dusty nods, and examines her more closely, perhaps trying to see if she's a niece he hasn't seen in years.

"I'll see you there?" she says.

Another smile and a nod.

She continues down the hallway.

Just past the coffee station is a door with a portal window giving a view to the kitchen. The backs of two women, one with short, silvery-brown curls, the other undoubtedly Raquel.

She didn't say she works here.

Winnow closes her eyes. She didn't sign up to work with a barely legal who might be having a heated fling with a man, that annoyingly, Winnow still has the hots for. She just wished Raquel didn't remind her of Emily.

She continues down the hall to the lobby, where a small, white cedar grows. On closer inspection, its planter is nestled into the stone floor, which looks designed around the tree. Three stories of plexiglass corridors wrap the lobby, and windows on the roof allow for natural light to reach the floor.

"Do you put Christmas lights on it in the winter?" a tiny, elderly woman with soft white hair, a mohair sweater, and a large pearl necklace asks a young woman with a long ponytail pulling luggage and escorting her and her husband through the lobby.

The husband, who's taller than his wife and equally white-haired, but with much less hair, says to the young woman, "What are you, about six-five?"

"Six-one and counting, sir."

"You play basketball?"

"Horseshoes are my game," she tells the man as they disappear around a corner, "I'm gonna be champ, just like my dad."

Winnow walks around the lobby, appreciating the art collection; birch bark scrolls, beaded items old and new, and murals of traditional life to modern graphics cover almost every surface.

The counter is quiet as she approaches, behind which, the door to the office is cracked, giving Winnow a peek inside.

It's him, Niigaanii.

He talks to someone out of sight.

Her eyes trace the curves of his arm. The faint aroma of skunk wafts from the office and tickles her nose. A wire rack holds pamphlets for the upcoming celebration. She grabs one and looks through the crack to see him pulling his shirt off. A surge of titillation reaches her fingers, and she tips the rack over.

"Oh!" She gulps.

He doesn't notice the clamor.

She eyeballs the lobby before resuming the trace of the muscles flowing across his shoulders and down his chest. She stuffs the pamphlets into the holder upside down and backward, while her eyes lick him as if he were a flavor of Indigenous popsicle she never tasted the likes of. Her pupils pause to nibble at a softness atop his hips before lapping their way to his stomach, kissing at the soft brown skin that disappears into his red boxers. If only she could get close enough to reflect just her eyes in the silver of his buckle.

She becomes aware she is staring too hard when she finds her gaze gnawing at the leather of his belt, wanting all things but him to be gone.

What's wrong with me?

She's never been one to engulf someone with her eyes like this before, in fact, she's always found this sort of ogling distasteful. But it had been a long time since she was with Chris. She suspected him unfaithful for three months and made excuses to not be intimate. There were normal reasons like menstrual cramps, indigestion, bloating, gas, tiredness, dizziness, and constipation. Then there were niche forager reasons. Like chigger bites on her hoohaa from cutting a whizz during a raspberry harvest, or the redness from stinging nettle on her arms she told him was painful and contagious when in fact it was helping the stiffness of her overworked wrists lessen. She finally got proof of Chris' infidelity when Emily's generously informative texts came in.

Niigaanii laughs and says something she can't make out. A shirt flies from the direction of whomever he's talking to and lands on his face.

A moment later, he appears in the doorway saying, "I'd rather not spend any time with that cook you hired, but I'll take her foraging if you sign off on the purchase order for the new freeze dryer for The Harvester as soon as she leaves."

The wind empties from Winnow's solar plexus, causing her to shrink to the size of a fly on the wall, regurgitating every inch of his delightful cuisine of form.

"Would you help our guest?" a woman says as she exits after him.

I wonder how far Mel is, maybe she can come back for me.

She fumbles her out phone and scrolls with no direction, attempting to appear unaware of the goings on inside the office.

He's not that good-looking. I mean, look at the gouge in the bottom of his chin. I thought it was a dimple, but it looks like he was attacked with a wood-whittling knife. And his hair? Yeah, it's long and pretty but look at how dusty it is. There's dust even in his eyebrows. He probably has a box of the stuff back there he rolls around in like a chinchilla before coming out.

She smiles.

Fuck it. I came here to have fun and this asshole isn't gonna stop me.

She exhales briskly, her ears hot with agitation and desire.

"Hi, I'm Winnow. I'm the cook for the event this week."

Niigaanii

"You're Winnow?"

"Yep."

"You're early," he manages as nonchalantly as possible.

"Uh-huh," she says, no sign of tossing him even the smallest smile.

"Did you hear...?" he points over his shoulder with his thumb at the conversation that took place behind him.

"Wish I hadn't."

"Ah. I guess that makes me..."

Winnow raises an eyebrow, "A gaping asshole?"

Niigaanii's mouth pauses agape before bouncing in a nervous chuckle, "Haven't heard anyone say gaped in a while."

"I'm bringing it back," she says. Her gaze drops to the logo on his fresh green t-shirt and reads, "Moozoons." Her eyes widen, "Little moose?"

"En', my sister Bibs just gave me this beauty. I was a bit ripe after collecting the zhigaag you helped with this morning." He smooths the front of his shirt with his hand, accentuating his pecks.

Bringing up the deceased skunk bounces him back to when they first exchanged words on the road earlier that morning. He hadn't stopped thinking about her all day.

Seriously though, Chris Brown?

He looks over her face, the features that captivated him earlier are now distracted by...

Is she checking me out?

He realizes his hands are pressed to his chest and lowers them.

She grabs the first thing in front of her, a pamphlet about the festival, "That was Bibs?" she says, flattening it against the counter and looking over its upside-down contents.

He chuckles.

Bibs emerges from around the corner, "My ears are ringing," she takes one look at Winnow, "You must be Winnow. I'm Bibs, nice to meet you in person."

"Aaniin, nice to meet you."

Bibs looks around the lobby, "Were you with someone?"

"My cousin Mel? She had a family emergency."

"I'm sorry to hear that. But you're okay with staying?"

Niigaanii feels Winnow's eyes upon him.

Uh oh.

"I think so," Winnow says.

"Great! Did Niigaanii check you in?"

"Not yet, we were just getting acquainted."

Bibs busies herself behind the computer, "You're in luck, we're booked solid through next Monday, but we had a cancellation in one of our suites this morning. Good thing you called ahead; I had a request right after."

Niigaanii takes the opportunity to busy himself with the bin behind the counter.

"Will I need to change rooms on Wednesday?" Winnow asks.

"Gaawiin, you'll be in 303 all week."

"Cool, chi-miigwech."

"Niigaanii's your guide this week," Bibs pats him on the shoulder to leave the bin alone, "It's his job to get you whatever you need, so don't be shy about asking."

"Great," Winnow says, the irony undetected by Bibs.

Niigaanii secures the neatness of the pen jar, flipping a few balls tip down.

Bibs doesn't skip a beat, "He'll take you foraging. We have plenty of staff and volunteers in the kitchen to work with the ingredients you bring in. He might even take you and a couple of our young men out to the big island to harvest."

"An island trip?" Winnow's eyes pop, "Are you coming with us?" she pleads.

"I wish I could, but my leg'd slow us down. Niigaanii'd have to carry me out of the bush on his back again," Bibs chuckles.

"You know I don't mind," he begs.

Niigaanii opens his mouth to say he's got enough help with the boys and that Winnow can hang back and take the lead in the kitchen, but Bibs keeps talking.

"Niigaanii will show you to your room and give you a tour of the kitchen when you're ready. Oh! You might need some wheels." Bibs produces a beaded keyring holding a kind of small key Winnow isn't familiar with, "You can take mine."

"What's this for?"

"Did you see the scooter by the door?"

"What? Really?"

"How are you getting home?" Niigaanii asks his sister.

"Harvey."

"I've never driven a scooter. Do I need a license?"

"Not if you stay on the rez." Bibs tosses her the keyring, "A girl's gotta have wheels. Have time for a quick lesson?"

At least I don't have to drive her everywhere.

***

"What's up with you, cuz? You're making my mural look like shit," Moozoons says.

Winnow... what was her last name again?

He gave her good reason to turn a cold shoulder, which was best for them both, but there was something familiar about her that made it hard for him to stop thinking about her.

Why'd she act so weird when she saw my shirt? Does she know Bruce?

Niigaanii stops staring across the parking lot. He pulls his mask down to his chin, "You know someone named Winnow?"

"Nah, that her?" Bruce motions to the scene Niigaanii was engrossed in, Winnow making valiant efforts to not topple on Bibs' scooter.

"Yeah. She's the cook Bibs hired for the festival."

"You like her, don't you?"

"She thinks I'm a jackass."

Bruce shoots a bright green can of spray paint through the air, flipping it end over end before it clunks in a bin, "Who doesn't?" he says.

Bibs' shouting of instructions is indistinct at a distance.

Bruce laughs, "Kidding cuz."

Niigaanii's pout pooches over the top of his mask. He replaces it over his nose and shakes a can before unleashing a thick pink mist.

When he stops spraying, he says, "You know, if this artist gig stops paying, you'd make a good shitty comedian."

Bruce rummages through a plastic tote bin holding a few dozen cans of spray paint on the folding table near the wall of the utility building, "You're just jealous nobody likes *your* jokes." He selects a purple and digs through a smaller bin for a nozzle to quickly cover a wide area.

"You wanna know what's not funny?" Niigaanii motions to Winnow, "Her fiancé is Chris Brown."

"The dude that made you the jail-bird?"

"That's him, the shit for brains. Stole my jacket and left it at that store he vandalized. I still don't know why he fucked me over. I'm just lucky the dishwasher broke and flooded the kitchen that night or I'd've had no alibi. Took me and Justen two hours to clean it up."

"You think she knows he did that shit?"

"I don't know. Bibs asked the same thing."

"You gonna tell her?"

Niigaanii discards his mask on the table, "Why would I do that?"

"I dunno, maybe cuz when we were like six you told Auntie Bertie you knocked over her beading table even though she blamed the cat."

Niigaanii laughs, "I forgot about that." He smooths away the chaos the mask's elastic band left on his head. "Looks like Bibs is done breaking her in. I better go do my job." He nods at the mural, "What comes next with this?"

"Gonna sketch in chalk." Bruce raps his knuckle on the mockup taped to the table. The graphic areas of shapes and colors they just finished are to be filled in with images of people from the community engaged with traditional foods. He talks about the mural while Niigaanii drifts off.

Am I going to tell her?

***

The hallways are chilled by Winnow's deadened stare as Niigaanii pulls her luggage to her suite. She insisted on carrying her foraging backpack and knife roll, mumbling something about not wanting bad energy on them. He assumes that her being unwelcomed by him, coupled with falling off the scooter, was the cause for her especially unpleasant mood.

I can do a few days of silence. It's better than making small talk the whole week.

He smiles as he rolls her luggage into the room and then steps outside the door, crossing his arms.

I'll be ordering the new freeze dryer for the truck in no time.

"You heard Bibs, I'm your guy if you need anything."

She reaches for the door, revealing scunned hands from the concrete, the look on her face matches the soreness of how her hands must feel.

It's now that Niigaanii doesn't see Chris Brown's fiancé. Standing before him is a human being in more than one kind of pain. His smile rots against his teeth.

You're an asshole. Don't be an asshole.

He slumps towards her and rests his hand on the doorframe near her face, "Can I get you anything?"

"Yeah," she says.

He raises his eyebrows at a potential chance to make amends for his behavior.

"Can you get out of here?"

"Yup," Niigaanii says, shoulders hunching towards his ears as he turns on his heels for the elevator.

Winnow

The room is cozy with two queen beds, a walk-in shower, a desk with the kind of lamp that's good for beading under, and a large set of windows.

She lies on her back at the foot of the bed closest to the windows, holding her scuffed, dusty hands in front of her face. With the task of digging the gravel from her palms complete, the silence of the human-made environment sinks in. There are no more unseen messages, no unplayed voicemails on her phone; the screen now cracked from dropping it on the bathroom floor after she read a text from Chris saying he misses her and is thinking of coming home early to see her in Rainy Bay.

She stayed true to ignoring his calls and messages, in the sense that she hadn't replied. But she also hasn't told him she left. Was she afraid of moving on? Would she have been more attractive to him if she bleached her hair? Wore revealing clothes? Boob job? Makeup? Would it have kept his attention? Would he have treated her any different? Was that on her? Pop culture made it seem so.

She squeezes her thirty-four C cups, "I love you, boobies."

If only she could find someone who doesn't mind a few bug bites in exchange for the bounties of a wild harvest, loves watching the seasons change, talks to plants, and loves animals as much as she does. Is that so much to ask? Oh, and how about a guy who appreciates brown skin and dark hair and not as a fetish?

Her pocket vibrates and she reluctantly fetches it out.

It's Melanie. *Hey, just stopped for gas. How's it going?*

Winnow texts back. *All good here. What about you? Love you.*

Love you too! I'm okay, just worried about my auntie. Also worried you're going to find Little Moose and snag up on him while I'm gone. LoL jk!

She doesn't tell Melanie she might have found him and he's the biggest asshole to come along since Chris. *Haha! That's the last thing I would do! Sending hugs to your auntie.*

Winnow doesn't mention the part about Melanie being lucky Niigaanii isn't an asshole otherwise it'd be impossible to not try her rusty snagging hand on him.

"I'm your guy," she says in a mocking tone, "Psssh, not even. Hi, I'm your guy, here to give you whatever you need."

She bites her lip and puts the phone back in her front pocket where it vibrated close to her nether regions. It crossed her mind she might be able to get the thing to vibrate continuously if she sent herself a series of quick texts. One minute was all she needed. Heck, call it forty seconds, call it good.

When her nether regions stop demanding the experiment be held, she gets another idea. Should she toy with Chris? She could tell him she's left him and there's a hot guy here, no, *two* hot guys she's already blown a dozen times each and she's in love with them both. What could she tell him to make him feel shitted on? She could post the sex pics Emily sent on social media, that way everyone would know what an asshole he is, and they would shit on him for her.

Instead of any of these options, she gets up to inspect the view and sees there's a balcony.

"Wow, cool."

The lake glitters in the near distance, beyond what looks like a series of garden plots and a darkish sandy beach. Kids play in the water, and a few families grill on the shore in the shade of mixed hard and softwoods. She leans on the wrought iron railing. A young family is working in the garden. Two small children run up and down the rows of vegetables, laughing.

She notices to the east side of the gardens, what looks like a three-seasons vegetable market stand. Two older women in skirts and sun hats fill paper bags with veggies from a basket and put the bags on the shelves of the market. One follows behind the other, tidying her work.

A heated breeze wafts in Winnow's face, bringing with it the cheer of song from birds happily bouncing under a row of small trees beneath the balcony. The smell of the beach causes the hair on her head to perk up like antennae, tuning in to memories of summer as a kid playing on the sandy beaches of Red Lake.

She takes a deep breath and releases it. She reaches into her pocket and pulls out a pouch, from which she takes a pinch of asemaa. She says a few words of love and care for Melanie's aunt and her family, before putting the asemaa on the ledge of the balcony. She'll put it by a tree later.

She puts an extra pinch down for herself and whispers, "Wiidookawishin daga." She's not in the habit of praying for herself, at least not for a while. She hasn't had the kind of problems she did as a younger woman. But with everything going on, she feels it's time to put in a personal ask.

Please help me this week to be a good person and do the best I can to help this community with the wonderful thing they're doing here. Please help me deal with this man and anyone who treats me unkind, with grace. Miigwetch.

She looks up, the big blue sky smiles down upon her, digging into her heart and lifting it a little farther out of the pit of sadness she wallowed in the last few days. Weeks. Months. With Melanie gone, it's just her for the week. After putting her asemaa down and clearing her heart and mind, the thought of being alone makes her happy. It's like she's starting a second life.

Winnow grabs hold of the railing and stretches with a side-to-side lean. A boogit slips out and she lowers her arms quickly to her sides. Two young men walking under the balcony snicker into their fists before disappearing around the building.

She tilts her chin upward to look dignified and scans the grounds, trying to project an heir of innocence.

Ground squirrels poke out of holes here and there across the field between the hotel and the gardens. She watches them tackle one another and dive in and out of holes until a small hawk swoops in looking for lunch and scaring the lot of them.

Halfway down the field, a dozen men work to erect a large canopy while another on an ATV stops every so often to drive orange markers into the ground for what looks like rows of parking or camping.

The sparkle of the water calls loudly and she returns inside to fetch her swimsuit from her luggage. She unzips the front pocket to toss her phone into it, the only safe bet she won't text Chris, but something is taking up the whole space. She pulls out a black box with a note on it that says, "YOLO!"

Uncovering the top reveals a purple dildo in the packaging.

"What the heck?" She flips over the note and reads, "Love, Mel."

Fuckin' Mel.

She grins.

Maybe later.

She chucks it on the spare bed.

***

Down by the beach, Winnow pulls sand between her toes. The evening sun sinks on the horizon, sending shades of pink and peach to kiss the tops of mellow, rolling waves. The last group of people pack into their car. The youngest protests in the shallows, kicking at the water and slapping his floater-adorned arms.

"Just five more minutes!" the boy yells.

"Jason, ambe! Let's go!"

"Just go without me!" he shouts.

"Now, Jason!"

"That lady will watch me!" He chin-nods at Winnow, who laughs.

"She don't wanna watch you!"

A woman, who Winnow assumes is Jason's mother, opens her car door to get out, prompting the boy to run as fast as he can out of the water. He gets wrapped in a towel and piles into the backseat to join what looks like a handful of siblings or cousins.

She looks up and down the beach. There's no one else around. She can hear the ATV in the distance, still zooming around the grounds. She rolls to her belly and pokes the sand with a twig and rests her chin in her hands, watching the last bit of sun absorb into the tips of trees along the shore as gulls swim through the sky.

Would be a shame not to go for a swim.

She pulls her shorts down and chucks them on her towel. Dipping a toe in, the water is warmer than the air and she dives under the waves. There's something about the way the water holds her that makes her feel protected, calm, and loved, melting away any remainder of stress. Even her beef with Niigaanii. All is forgotten as her skin meets the water. She tips her head back to cover all but her face, and floats, welcoming the wind into her lungs, the sounds of the underwater realm in her ears.

An eagle flies overhead, *Keep going*, the eagle's encouragement hugs her warmly.

Back on the beach, she dusts sand from her bottom with her towel and bends to pull up her shorts.

"I got away from one asshole and I may be stuck with another, but this week is going to be good," she says to the wind.

"Who's the other asshole?"

She spins to see Niigaanii.

How long was he watching? Did he see my ass?

She sinks into her towel.

"I'm kidding. Are you hungry? I brought food."

He sits in the sand next to her and holds out a paper bag.

Her stomach growls, "What is it?"

"Walleye sandwich and some veggies from the garden. Made it myself, except for the buns. Those are from Buns by Bev, a local baker." He smiles at her; he seems warmer than earlier.

The tenseness in her unwinds.

"I'll let you eat your dinner," he says and stands up, "I'm taking a couple of youngsters out to harvest tomorrow. It'd be nice if you'd come." He pats sand from his pants, "Please come."

She sits quietly, staring at the lake, and takes out a jar of wild plum jam from her backpack, the last one with her failed business stamp on it. She spreads some on the bun, "What time?"

"One o'clock, but I could use some help in the kitchen before then, say, eight?"

She nods.

"What's that?"

She screws the lid on and hands him the jar, "Wild plum."

His eyes widen as he reads the label, "Wild at Hart." He looks at her, "Where'd you get this?"

"I made it."

"You made this?"

Big surprise this doofus thinks I can't make a jar of jam.

She smiles and says, "My last name puts the Hart in Wild at Hart."

Niigaanii

The next morning, Niigaanii sits on his porch eating oatmeal, waiting for the sun to pierce the horizon.

"Winnow Hart. I knew she looked familiar. I only had eyes for Cindy back then and heck, I wouldn't've noticed if what's her name, the blondie from the beach show came into the restaurant." He licks his spoon, "I like dark hair anyhow."

At the bottom of the stairs, Mr. Puppers munches his oats from the N mug. The one with a C sits in a box with yard debris near the shed.

"I didn't know they were a couple at the time. The day she came into the restaurant was the day Chris stole my jacket and my life. I wish I knew what one had to do with the other."

The dog snorts into his breakfast.

"I don't know why I froze when I saw the jar last night."

Niigaanii's oatmeal fills a plain, brown bowl. The little glass vessel sits next to him, garnering an occasional glance, "What was I supposed to say? I've been carrying this around for a year, no biggie. She must think I'm a jerk, huh?"

The dog lifts his head, a few drops of gravy added as a special treat, hang from his bottom lip.

"I'm a little anxious for her to remember me, but that doesn't mean I like her."

The two make eye contact.

Mr. Puppers gives a quiet *woof!* and trots to a patch of grass and stubby mint plants. He flops down and smears his face and wriggles his body on the green-earth floor. He tucks his front legs under and plows along until his chest is streaked green, his fur aromatic.

"Your right. I'm going to enjoy myself this week whether or not our guest is engaged to a giant shithead."

Mr. Puppers yawns and rolls over, conveying his confidence in Niigaanii's ability to sort the situation out.

"Right. Well, in any case, I better pick some miinaan for Delores' muffins. Naagaj, Mr. Puppers."

Winnow

Winnow blow-dries her hair enough to not be drippy. She gently scrunches it, encouraging body into the locks, paying no mind to the silenced message banners popping up across her phone on the bathroom counter. She ties her hair in a loose bun and notices her bangs will need trimming soon. That or it's time to let them finish their stretch to hit behind her ears.

Before walking out of the bathroom she looks at herself.

Positive self-talk, Winnow.

It took a decade to break the habit of self-sabotaging inner dialogue but giving herself positive affirmations was entirely new and felt like it required some new superpower to achieve.

If only I had a can of wild spinach.

"This is a good day. I can make this day good. I want this day to be a good day."

She slips on a pair of white, closed-toe sneakers, picks her phone up off the counter, and seeing none of the notifications are from Melanie, stuffs it in her back pocket.

"String the moments together and make something beautiful," she tells herself before leaving the room. In the lobby, she finds Bibs and another woman, Florence, her name tag says, discussing the status of the rooms.

"We've got people coming from Oklahoma, New Mexico, and Oregon today."

Winnow finds the flyers for the week's event.

"Mind if I take one of these?"

"Go for it," Bibs says," her square cheeks lifting her dark frame glasses in a warm, heartful smile like the one Niigaanii gave her on the road the previous morning.

"You've got a nice smile," Winnow says without thinking about it.

"It's my mom's," Bibs pulls a picture from under the counter of a family standing by a seventies model car: Bibs about five wearing red overalls; her mom, smiling and looking like Bibs does now; her dad, wearing a purple bandanna and choker; and Niigaanii, barefoot and showing a missing front tooth.

"What's her name?"

"Marybeth," Bibs puts the picture back, "Can we get you anything to make you more comfortable? How's your room?"

"I'm good, the view in the room is incredible. I'm just on my way to meet Niigaanii in the kitchen."

"Go right ahead," Bibs points down the hall.

"Miigwech."

***

The kitchen is empty but for Niigaanii at a stainless-steel counter along the far wall, his back towards her. Several awning windows line the room, the one nearest him open with no screen.

Approaching him from behind, she attempts to repress the shapes of him she saw the morning before, but it's no use. His apron is pulled snugly at his waist, accentuating the trapezoid of his torso. His t-shirt, although loose-fitting, can't conceal the muscular nature of his back and shoulders from her mind's eye, which stares in an unblinking stupor.

There's the sound of rushing water, and he begins moving in a gyrating motion, his pelvis bumping on the steel counter in front of him in quick beats.

Her pulse quickens, creating a bright hum in her skull that radiates out her eyes, making blurry her surroundings.

Mel's present.

She bites her lip and turns to leave. The weakness in her knees causes the duffle bag of ingredients she brought to slide from her shoulder and land in the crook of her arm with a loud clank of glass, stopping her wet in her tracks.

He turns to inspect his visitor, "Morning," he says and resumes his gyrating.

It takes two breaths to steady herself before floating to the counter where he shakes a large colander of blueberries over a sink basin. Insects and spiders attempt to crawl from the splash. A few small twigs and leaves remain to be plucked.

"Did you pick all of those this morning?" she says.

"This is just what's left," he smiles, his waist bumping the edge of the sink firmly enough to polish the steel, "I ate the rest from the bush."

Her knees wobble. And then the pictures of Chris and Emily charge through her mind.

Why? When will you let me be?

And then comes Raquel's story of having her pants down in the woods and she can't help but think of Raquel and Niigaanii out there doing who knows what.

She slumps.

Gross. I don't want to know what you were eating out there.

Her legs firm, her butt cheeks slap together to ward off intruders and her plumbing tightens to prevent even the tiniest of drips. She gives him and his black denim apron the stink eye until noticing little purple appliqué flowers and colorful ribbons sewn across the front. The hem nearest her reveals the embroidered name, Marybeth.

His mom's. Her butt cheeks relax slightly. How bad could a guy be who wears his mother's apron? Chris wouldn't be caught dead in an apron of any kind.

"This looks like it took an hour to pick by yourself."

"Time well spent, and I had company."

Company?

There's no one else in the kitchen, "You mean the plants?" She sets her duffel bag of dried wild things on the far end of the counter.

He smiles, "Well them too, but I was talking about my friend with one and a half ears, a quiet disposition, and all he ever asks me for is my leftovers."

He's got a nice sense of humor.

Niigaanii stops working to help a spindly, green-legged spider out the window without a screen on it. A gentle observance flows between them as he does this, him observing the spider, and Winnow observing him.

After a minute of her breathing down his neck, he says, "I take them from their homes, it's the least I can do."

Her heart flutters like a memengwa set free from a jar. Chris' wanton killing of spiders and insects was a point of contention for years and turned into one of the things that made their relationship feel doomed, her heart compromised.

A stray wave of hair escapes his ponytail and traces along his cheek, landing at his eye. He pushes at it with the back of his hand but is unsuccessful in sticking it behind his ear.

His hair looks so soft.

She wants to help him but knows it's inappropriate. Standing within arm's reach, the brown of his eyes reveals a reddish-purple tinge same as his hair, which is a shade lighter than black. A triangular-shaped scar the size of a piece of hominy sits above his left eyebrow. His face and nose are wide to match his shoulders. Peachfuzz covers his face, an indication that hair doesn't grow in the absence of a razor. A quick scan of his arms shows no hair grows there either. She, however, has plenty of arm hair.

Winnow empties the ingredients from her bag. She pauses to open a jar filled with wild rice she harvested with a friend from Leech Lake last ricing season. She takes a deep breath, her eyes closed. She watches the rice grow on the water with anticipation and awe, feels the sunshine and sore muscles from the weeks of harvest, and smells the smoke of the fire and the buttery-nutty scent of parching rice.

Her stomach growls. Follows is a hunger in her heart, an ache that leaves her spirit throbbing with unmet longing. She closes the lid, sealing the memories away for later.

"Sorry if I came off as an ass yesterday," he says.

She smiles, nods, "I've been in a mood myself," and before she can stop herself, adds, "I moved out of my ex-fiancé's house yesterday, but I haven't told him I've left him yet."

Niigaanii raises an eyebrow, "How long were you together?"

"Four years. But he's been cheating on me. And he's *really* a gaping asshole."

The lift of his brow softens.

Feeling lighter than it has in ages, her body bounces with a full laughter. A blueberry jumps the colander and skips across the counter. She catches it and rolls the little blue ball in her palm before leaning towards him to return it. Her forearm brushes the back of his arm, and he coughs.

"This is enough for Delores' muffins for our elder brunches next couple of days, but the way she stuffs her muffins, we'll need more soon."

"Bibs said you've got the best blueberries around," She pops one into her mouth.

"En'," He clears his throat, "These are good, but they're not the best."

She smiles, "She also said to tell you if I need anything,"

"Can't say she didn't."

"I'm gonna need proof Rainy Bay has the best blueberries."

Niigaanii

Niigaanii studies the dried items Winnow stacked on the counter.

Nettle, dried juneberries, violet, lilac, and apple blossoms, some kind of dried leaves, maybe wild spinach, ramps, pickled purslane, wild bergamot, chaga jelly, hazelnuts, acorn, and manoomin flours. Not bad.

He makes his way back to his berries.

After she's finished unpacking, Winnow reads from the festival flyer, "Wow, looks like you're gonna have food demos, a garden market and tour, a canoe build and race, a concert, lacrosse, basketball, and horseshoe games, an art market and then the big dinner on Friday."

Niigaanii sets the colander on a towel at the edge of the sink. He clears twigs from the drain and puts them in a compost bin beneath the counter. He dries his hands on a towel hanging at his waist and says, "Alright."

"Alright, what?"

"I'll take you to the most delicious blueberries in the world, but you're going to need camping gear."

"An overnight trip?"

"We canoe to the big island, then it's a short portage to the wet-lands and a half-hour hike to the berry camp. We have to wait for those youngsters I mentioned to join us though. They'll be here this afternoon. If we want to make the most of the daylight, we pick this evening and again tomorrow before we return."

She bites the corner of her lip and he can tell she does her best to sound confident, "I have gear."

"Good," He unties his apron, hangs it up, and pulls the green compost bag from the bin, "You won't be needing that," he says, tying the bag and offering it to her in exchange for the flyer, "I'll show you around while we wait for the boys to get here."

She takes the bag, "For me? Aww, you shouldn't have."

He grins, "Welcome to Rainy Bay. We'll start at the gardens."

***

Outside in the parking lot, Niigaanii smiles and chuckles to himself as Winnow lifts the compost bag into the back of the truck without being directed, before walking to stand by the passenger door waiting for entry as if it was nothing. As if he's welcoming of women in his personal space since Cindy.

He motions to the scooter, "We could take that."

"Gimme your keys, I'll drive this rig," she says.

He chuckles and unlocks the doors.

She's the first woman in almost two years to enter his truck without him intending on removing her as fast as possible. It's not like he's invited her because he's trying to woo her. Is he?

For a split second, he'd taken Chris' side after hearing Winnow left without saying a word. It was too similar to the way Cindy left without even a note. But he never cheated on Cindy and he wasn't an asshole to her. At least he likes to think he wasn't.

***

Down in the community garden, Niigaanii leans on a shady post of the market stand and watches Winnow tag behind the elder gardeners, Susie and Viola. Her shorts are stained on the front from spilling the contents of the kitchen scrap bag while dumping it in the compost bin.

He smiles at the image of her gasping, shouting *shit!* and shaking the spinach leaves from her sandals, but recovering quickly to grab a pitchfork and turn the pile over.

Several times a week Niigaanii brings kitchen scraps and tends to the compost bin. He does other tasks as requested but knows to stay off Susie and Viola's toes; they're both very particular and often disagree on garden protocol.

And yet there she is, still in tow after nearly an hour, currently helping them weed around the potatoes. The voracity of her questioning about gardening has prompted them to graciously rely on the knowledge of the other to satiate her thirst for knowledge.

Another fifteen minutes pass before she approaches him, her bangs stuck to her head with sweat. A smear of dirt adorns her cheek from wiping at a biting fly with a dusty glove. Her face looks kissed by the sun, her freckles darker than the hour before. The flush of her skin from physical exertion coupled with sweat and the fact that she's smiling, sets his heart racing.

"What a treasure. They are the sweetest couple," she says, "and so knowledgeable."

He looks to the women. They gaze over rows of peppers, Susie pats Viola on the shoulder. Viola reaches up and holds Susie's hand there. They exchange a smile before getting back to work.

Just then, Niigaanii's cousin Jay appears behind him, "Hey Cousin, who's your friend?"

"Boozhoo, I'm Winnow," she says, dusting her hand off on her dirty shorts before offering it to him.

He shakes it, "Oh, you're the cook, eh? I'm Jay, Niigaanii's wiser and more handsome cousin."

She chuckles, "Yeah, that's me."

"Ripe and crusty is more like it," Niigaanii says, "Whuddyup to, cuz?"

"Came to borrow a hose for the carwash."

"NeeJee's SkweeJees opening soon?" Niigaanii asks.

"NeeJees SkweeJees?" Winnow laughs loudly and throws a hand over her mouth, "That's a great name."

Niigaanii pauses to take in the first big laugh he's heard from her. He likes the way she looks when she laughs like that, her eyes squinting and creating wrinkles at the corners, her posture less tense than the day before. He directs his attention back to Jay.

"I know it's a good name, I came up with it," Jay beams, "Actually, I'm doing a carwash to help fund the carwash. You two should stop by, be out by the Trading Post," he says and moves along to finesse Susie and Viola into borrowing a hose.

Niigaanii watches as Winnow walks behind the market stand and throws the water pump handle up and down. It's the first time he's taken more than a glimpse at the build of her body. She's the kind of athletic you get from physical work and being on your feet all day.

She drinks from the forceful spray of the water pump and then lifts her head up and slicks her hair back like she's done it a thousand times. The front of her shirt is wet and clings to her breasts.

Niigaanii faces the hotel, "It's almost one. The canoes are at my place. You wanna head there to help me load?" He winces and turns back around in time to see her lift the bottom half of her shirt to wring it out, showing her slick tan belly in the process. "Or we could stop by your room first. So you can change, I mean, if you like."

"Sounds good to me."

Winnow

They drive across the field towards the hotel with the windows down, the heat of the afternoon sun blasting Winnow's hair dry. Niigaanii slows the truck to talk to a couple of kids carrying handmade lacrosse sticks.

"You two ready for the game?" Niigaanii asks, pulling up beside them.

"Yeah, we're done practicing, but Natalie lost her shoe, so we have to go back and find it," the boy says.

Natalie looks embarrassed and mad. She's wearing one jelly sandal. Dusty toes on her barefoot grip at the grass, "Markus was throwing dirt at me, so I ran, and I don't know where it is," she says and gives him a dirty look.

"Nuh-uh," Markus says.

"Yah-huh," Natalie retorts.

Markus smiles guiltily and shrugs.

The sun hits something reflective in the field and Winnow points with her lips, "Is that it?"

The girl investigates the distance before pulling Marcus to follow her. Out in the field, she sits on the ground to replace the jelly. The children wave and give a thumbs-up before racing toward the gardens.

***

Back in her room, Winnow brushes her teeth and video chats with Melanie.

"Don't take this the wrong way, Win, but I kinda thought you'd've called Chris to forgive him by now. I'm proud of you."

"I wasn't sure myself," Winnow says and sticks her tongue out to brush it.

"You let that asshat know he's coming home to an empty house yet?"

She pats her face dry and inspects a pimple on her chin, "No, and I'm kinda wigging out."

"Why?"

"He texted saying he misses me and might leave his work trip early and come see me in Rainy Bay."

"What?"

"I think he's full of shit and fishing to see if I got the photos, and I'm not getting pulled into that. I'm trying to enjoy myself and do my job. He'll figure it out when he gets home. By then, you'll be back, and we'll be hittin' the road."

"Be there soon as I can," Melanie says and blows Winnow a kiss.

"Oh yeah," Winnow says, "Guess who my guide is?"

"No clue."

"The cute guy from the road."

"No way!"

"Yes way, and that's not all."

"Go on."

"We're gonna camp on an island to harvest blueberries."

"Camp?"

"It's an overnight trip."

"Nuh-uh!"

"Yuh-huh."

***

Five minutes later, Winnow lay on the bed staring at the shiny threads that create a white-on-white floral pattern in the comforter. She told Niigaanii she'd meet him in the lobby in twenty and it's been fifteen.

"I can't go camping with this guy, can I? Can I call you Peter?" she says, picking up the yet un-boxed dildo. In resisting him, she's adorned Pete's box with messages like, "Play with me," and, "Don't think twice, I play nice."

"You prefer Pete?" she says, "You got it," and adds his name in marker. She gives him a square-face smile and flowing hair. Through the open balcony door, the sound of that Native rock band from the seventies' top love song starts in.

She bounces her foot, "I definitely can't go if I like him." She scrolls through the chat with Chris and Emily, "But Chris would be so mad if he knew I was camping with another man. I should do it—and do him, Niigaanii—and take pictures and send them to Chris."

"Ew, sorry you had to hear that, Pete," she says and tosses him onto the spare bed.

She selects all the images. Her thumb hovers over the delete button. She hits it and her lips flap over a loud release of air. Victorious, she puts the phone down. She then remembers a copy of every texted image is saved in her phone's photo album. She'll need to delete them there as well.

"Shit."

Unable to look at them again, if only to delete them once and for all, she says, "Who cares what Chris would think?"

She gets up and slings her hiking pack on, "Pete, I'm going camping. Don't do anything I wouldn't do."

***

In the lobby, a woman about Winnow's age holds up the line at the check-in counter.

"I made my reservation months ago and I just drove from Oregon to be here."

"I'm really sorry. We have on-site camping," Bibs says, her glasses now low on her nose, her face sweaty.

"You can stay in my room if you want," Winnow says before realizing who the woman is, "Hey, you're that MMA fighter."

The woman swivels in Winnow's direction, sending a few braids to slap on the shoulder straps of her backpack. She sizes Winnow up quietly.

"I have an extra bed and a great view," Winnow says, "I'll be gone camping tonight, so you'll have it to yourself."

"You're going camping?" Bibs asks.

"Your brother's taking me to the island."

Bibs tugs her glasses loose, "He is?"

"Mhm."

"Why would you let me stay with you?" The woman says to Winnow, "I could be a weirdo."

"Well, I'm definitely a weirdo," Winnow says.

The woman laughs, "Sure. Why the hell not? What else am I gonna do?"

***

Winnow finds Niigaanii in his truck under the portico. Two young men sit over the wheel wells, their backpacks beside them.

Oh no.

It's the young men who walked under her balcony the day before.

I wonder if they'll remember me.

She opens the door and Niigaanii gives introductions through the rear window, "Winnow, this is Derek and Michael. Guys, this is Winnow."

They give a nod and a quiet, "Hey."

"Hey," Winnow says, jumping in.

"We need to get gas," Niigaanii says.

She looks through the window to the boys.

I don't think they recognize me.

They pull out from the portico.

BRAAAT! A palm fart from the back of the truck is followed by snickering.

Niigaanii looks at them and then at Winnow.

"Boys," she says and busies herself with the scenery.

***

At the Trading Post, she peeks around the end of an aisle to see Niigaanii chatting with the clerk who checked her and Melanie out the day before.

"Hey, Shannon," Niigaanii says.

Shannon, a thirty-something Native woman with freshly ironed and sprayed split-level bangs, shrugs, "Forty-five," she says, referring to the gas Niigaanii pumped.

"Where's Merle?" he says, offering cash.

"I heard you're being nice to her. You like her?" Shannon nods at Winnow.

Winnow grabs a bag of puffed sweet potato chips and looks down the aisle to where the youngsters grab cheeseburgers from a cooler.

"Who said that? Was it Jay?" Niigaanii says.

Another shrug from Shannon.

"Bibs hired her to help with the festival."

"She's in town, you know," Shannon says.

"Who?"

"Cindy."

The sound of the young men giggling and the palpable awkwardness at the counter diverts her out of earshot. She walks to where the boys are stuffing cheeseburgers into the microwave just long enough to warm them for rapid consumption.

"That's all you got?" Derek asks Michael.

Michael slams an empty wrapper down on the table and puts another cheeseburger into the microwave.

After the rest of her crew exits the store, Winnow makes her way to the register and finds a bottle of tea.

"Boozhoo," she says to Shannon.

Shannon doesn't reply.

That's weird. She was friendly last time I was here.

"You working with Niigaanii?" Shannon says, scanning Winnow's things.

"Yeah. We're gonna go pick blueberries on the island."

The woman stops scanning, "Did he tell you how he got that scar on his face?"

"I just met him. I don't really know anything about him."

"His dad drove him and his sister off the cliff when we were kids."

Winnow remembers seeing a cliff on the lakeshore in the distance while at the beach the day before. She looks through the store's front window. Niigaanii lets down the truck gate to let the guys into the back, but they hop in over the wheel wells and Michael says something to Niigaanii that makes him shake his head and smile as he shuts the gate.

Winnow pays for her items and offers Shannon and her raised eyebrow, a, "Miigwech."

Niigaanii

*H*ow did this happen?

Niigaanii shakes his head in disbelief as Winnow hangs out of the truck, laying her head on her arm and letting the early afternoon air bubble up onto her face.

It's a mixture mix of wet-cool from the shade of plant cover and warmth from the quickly heating day. He'd be hanging out in it himself if he wasn't keeping an eye on the two youngsters in the back.

How did you get in my truck?

It boils him to think of Cindy knowing anything about his life now.

In watching Winnow, who looks like she's genuinely enjoying herself without the need to say anything to him, his frustration dissipates into the wind and he finds himself aroused by her self-contained contentedness with being alive in the moment.

How did Bibs talk me into this?

The heat of his loins combined with the warm wind on his face makes his mouth dry.

"Pazz the vazz?" He points his dry lips to the glove box.

Winnow finds a tiny brown jar of unidentifiable goop with "vazz" scrawled on the lid, the v smudged away from contact with said goop.

"You want this... azz?" she says.

He throws his eyes at her and shifts into a more upright posture.

She smiles and waves the little jar in the air.

"Daga," he says, and holds out his hand.

She tosses it to him, "What is that stuff, anyway?"

"Special recipe for ultra-soft smoochers," he says before realizing he's telling her *he* has soft smoochers. This makes his mouth feel extra dry, and he grabs the bottle of tea in the middle console and takes a good guzzle.

Ahh, that's good.

"That one's mine," Winnow says.

Niigaanii stuffs the bottle into the holder and pulls the neck of his shirt up to wipe the dribbles running over his chin, "You go by 'if you lick it, it's yours' rules?" he says, "Because if you do, it's mine now."

She attempts to hide her smile in her hand and returns to the window.

Did that sound how I think it did? Am I flirting with her? Remember, the less you say, the better.

***

At the end of the long dirt driveway to Niigaanii's cabin, the boys are the first out of the truck.

"Reh, stinks back there!" Derek has his shirt pulled up over his face, laughing as he leaps out.

"Nah, shut up. Must be your upper lip." Michael follows him out in a perfectly unhurried manner but is unable to hide his embarrassment. He punches his brother on the shoulder.

"Would you guys bring the canoes down to the shore?" Niigaanii asks Derek and Michael, "You remember where it is?"

"Yeah, down the path behind the cabin," Derek says.

"Miigwech," Niigaanii says as the young men head off, the older moving faster than the younger, who holds his stomach as he walks.

Where'd she go?

Niigaanii walks around his truck and finds Winnow squatting by a patch of wild mint plants. A grasshopper pelts low on her bare shin. She stands and wipes the ink left behind with the sock of her other foot. She smiles, "I'm looking forward to talking to some plants today," she says, "Plants are some of my favorite people."

"Mine too," he says and then stops himself from saying any of the fifty things about plants he'd like to say right now.

The less she knows about you, the better. Don't take her inside your house. Don't show her The Harvester. Get her down to the lake and to the island where you'll have lots of space.

"Is there someplace I can fill up my water pack?" she says.

Shit.

"Inside the cabin, help yourself."

Winnow

S mells are ushers of love and sustenance; they gather and sew you through time and provide your spirit with markers of the path you take.

As Winnow enters the cabin, the smell of manoomin dust ensconced in the walls like marrow in bones, hanging herbs releasing their essences, and dried things filling jars on shelves winding the room, she feels like an exposed hermit crab stumbling into a shell that's a perfect fit.

The front door opens to the kitchen. She sets the water pack on the counter and walks down the hall, following the trail of jars at eye level. The kind of love required here, strikes her deep desire to connect with another human being over such a love like a tuning fork.

Her dry mouth reminds her why she went inside in the first place. She goes back to the kitchen. Before filling her water pack, she picks the first empty vessel from the cupboard, a pint jar, and paying no attention to the lid lying face down beside it, gets a drink from the faucet. She puts the jar on the counter and fills her pack.

The porch creeks a greeting as she steps outside.

Who is this man and why did he tell his sister he didn't want to spend any time with me? What would make him feel that way without knowing anything about me? Does he know something about me?

***

Down a short path to the lake, Winnow catches her first glimpse at the island.

"That out there," Niigaanii says, pointing with his chin and lips, "is where the best blueberries are. Plenty more than blueberries out there though."

"Like what?"

"Behind that island is a smaller one where the spirits who watch over this place and our people live. The name Rainy Bay comes from out there, where the spirits push and pull the water around. One minute it'll be the sunniest day, and the next you're drowing in your socks."

Winnow listens quietly. A small flock of lake gulls hop on the smooth stone beach, nipping at one another and beaking between the rocks.

"You guys go first," Niigaanii says to Derek and Michael, "We'll follow you down."

The boys pull their canoe down the short hill to the water.

"Ready?" he asks her.

The tips of the trees on the island, bend gently with the wind, like fingers on a hand beckoning her over.

"Eya'."

Niigaanii

The water is calm as they row their way toward the island. It's the kind of quiet that's filled with life. She runs her fingers through the water and smiles.

It doesn't go unnoticed by Niigaanii, who has a good view of her from his station in the back of the canoe.

"What is it?" he says.

"I was just thinking, it's kind of stupid, but all of this," she motions at the quietly alive world around them, "is like a great score of music, of happiness, love. This is a good rhythm. This right here, this is a good jam. It's like a track I could play over and over again."

He smiles, "It's like recognizing a heartfelt classic when you hear it even if you don't know the lyrics."

"Exactly."

"Kind of like this," he says and hums a verse of a recognizable seventies song before belting, "Go-ing to the bath-room in my miii-iiind."

At this eruption, Winnow grabs onto the seat of the canoe to catch her balance.

Their combined laughter that follows, adds to the music of life stirring around and within, moving spirit and flesh to exhilaration.

He can't help but be attracted to the way she moves through the world; if his wood were a tree, it would be growing leaves and budding flowers right about now.

After a few minutes of rowing, she turns to him, "Do you know my cousin, Melanie?"

"Can't say I know any Melanies."

"Is your name Moozoons?"

He laughs, "What?"

"Your shirt."

"Moozoons is my cousin. I do love hanging out in the places where Moozoog frequent though."

"Where's that?"

"You're looking at it. This here," he taps the canoe, "is my favorite way to see the world."

"I have a canoe," Winnow says.

"Yeah?"

"Yeah. But it needs some work."

"What kind of work?"

She pauses, "The kind that can patch bullet holes."

"You get people shooting at you? I heard someone got shot at again over in Wisconsin during spearing season."

"Nothing like that. I kept it near my garden and my ex dinged it up shooting at my squashes. He thought there was something wrong with the bumpy ones, so he lined them on top of my belly-up canoe."

That's fucked up, but you can't ask about her ex.

"We had a big yard and some distance from our neighbors, but still in the city limits. Someone called the cops and Chris told them he didn't hear anything. Anyway, that was last year, a week before ricing season."

Don't engage.

Niigaanii shakes his head.

"I managed to save some of the seeds," she says and untucks from her shirt a tiny glass jar necklace holding a single seed, "I keep this one here to remind me of the promise of new growth beyond a shitty experience."

Segue. Segue.

"And now you're in Rainy Bay."

"I almost didn't come. I figured it would be good for me. Recharge, make new good memories. It was draining with him, Chris."

"So, he's a bloodsucker?"

Winnow laughs, "You get leeches in this lake?"

Finally.

"Sometimes, but they never bother me. I'm faster than any leech. I bet I could catch that one swimming by you there." Before she realizes what's happening, he's lunged forward and reaching across her, plunging his arm into the water. He pulls up a ten-inch spotted leech, his fist gripping at its middle as it thrashes wildly.

"Ewwww, oh my god!" Winnow laughs.

The boat shifts and he drops to a sitting position to steady it. He chucks the leech back into the water where it swims off on the hunt and he washes his hands in the lake.

Her laughter turns into snorts and tears well up in her eyes.

"Don't worry, I always carry salt when I come out here, so if you need someone to sprinkle any on your toes, I'm your guy."

I'm your guy? Ugh, that sounds weird.

Winnow wipes her eyes, "I'm no stranger to that. When I was a kid, we'd get home from the boat landing and my mom would send us to the bathtub with a bottle of salt, and I remember being surprised by the amount of blood that would stream into the tub when those rubbery little creatures finally came off." She shakes her head, "You wouldn't believe some of the stuff I did as a kid."

"Oh? Like?"

"Well. I never realized until early adulthood that a lot of people have never found a wood tick on them. On the other hand, when I was a kid, sometimes I would find one on my head and put it back so I could find it again later like it was a game."

Niigaanii's laughter brings attention from the boys.

"Settle down!" Derek shouts.

"Good to know I've got a master tick finder in my company. It's always good to have one around."

Winnow smiles and faces the front of the canoe.

Did that sound like I want her to look me over naked for wood ticks?

Winnow

Around the backside of the island, they come to a small sandy bay. A smaller island sits opposite the bay. The boys are a few minutes behind but visible.

Winnow hops from the nose of the canoe and pulls it and Niigaanii ashore. They unload their gear and take turns relieving themselves in the bushes.

"I couldn't see it rowing up," Winnow says emerging from the bush and motioning to the smaller island.

He nods, "From all surrounding shores it looks like it's a part of this one." He whispers and puts asemaa in the water between the two islands.

Derek pulls the canoe up onto the shore, his brother lying in the middle on top of their packs.

"What's wrong with him?" Niigaanii asks.

"He's a sore winner," Derek says.

"Nah, I'm okay," Michael says, and rolls off, landing halfway in the water.

Derek laughs.

The crew portages through the shade of a mixed forest to a large pond.

A few beavers busy themselves with the upkeep of the waterway. They tend to the blue flag irises growing on a floating mat and stop to munch on rhizomes.

At the other side of the pond, Michael tosses his backpack to the ground and sits down, folding himself over it.

"Alright, what's going on? Michael, are you okay?" Niigaanii says.

The boy groans.

"I think he has a cheeseburger belly," Winnow says, "I saw him eat three of the things before we left the Trading Post."

"He ate four," Derek chimes in, "I only ate two, but I feel sick to my stomach too."

"You guys shouldn't eat that garbage," Niigaanii says.

More groans.

"Michael, do you want to wait it out or do we need to call Harvey to come get you with the motorboat?"

Michael lifts his head, "What if it's contagious, you know, the virus."

"Cheeseburger virus," Derek says.

"Shit," Niigaanii says, "He's right, they both have symptoms. We can't have them harvest for the festival like this. Derek, do you have a cell phone?

"Yeah, but there's no reception."

"Mine worked at the bay," Winnow says.

"All right, you two stay here while I'll show Winnow the way to the campground. I'll be back to get you to the bay and wait for Harvey."

He wants to camp with just the two of us?

Niigaanii walks her a short distance down the trail and points to a clearing ahead, "That's where we camp. Are you okay with setting up while I get the guys back to the beach and wait for Harvey?"

"There's so many chanterelles here," she says, her eyes darting from one orange funnel to the next.

He glances at them, "They're a little small. Another day, maybe? What if we harvest them on our way out tomorrow?" He smiles at her, sending her heart into her throat. "I gotta get the cheeseburger bandits back to the beach. Are you gonna be okay?" The gentleness in his voice is inviting.

The bright aroma of pines permeates her nose, their vibrancy expanding a great feeling of wellness inside of her.

"Yeah, I'll be okay."

Niigaanii

N iigaanii returns to find the camp quiet, his tent erected, his gear inside. He sets up his bedding and digs out his fishing pole.

"Thanks for setting me up," he says, finding her returning on one of two outbound trails opposite the one leading into camp.

She drops an armful of firewood and motions behind her, "What's with the cave back there?"

"People go there to talk to the spirits."

She nods.

"I'm gonna try and catch us some dinner," he says, "just down there." He motions to the third trail.

***

A half-hour later, walleye in hand, Niigaanii finds her tending a fire. A pan sits on coals to the side of the flames.

"Never doubted you," she says, seeing him walking up, smiling.

"I see that."

He lets her take the walleye from him to prepare it for the pan.

***

Niigaanii's effort to devour the best walleye sandwich he's ever eaten is disturbed by the jar of plum jam sitting on a stump nearby, its contents smothering his sandwich.

"Wild plum," he says, "one of my favorites."

"Mine too."

The walleye is juicy, with blackened edges. She added a pinch of finely cut flat cedar to the fillet, and along with the jam, the sandwich was topped with dock leaves, giving it a sweet and tangy flavor profile.

She works on her own meal with a hungry gobble and catches him smiling at her, "What?"

"You're made of wild plum, walleye, and wild dock."

She takes another bite and pulls out a bone, "Today, I suppose. Yesterday I was cheese curls and sparkling water."

"I was three-day-old naboob and grilled cheese. I have no excuses."

"Sounds good," she says.

"Still some left."

She doesn't think I'm inviting her to dinner, does she? Who would want five-day-old fish soup?

He turns his head, represses a facepalm, and then adds, "I always cook too much, after working in commercial kitchens. It's hard to cook for one."

Not a bad save.

"I always cook too much, too."

"Have you worked in restaurants?"

"Yeah, but more so in catering. A couple of years back, I was saving money and spending my free time storing my harvests. Last year I found a kitchen to use in a health food store. My plan was to produce baked goods, jams, and pickled wild veggies, and use their large-scale freeze dryer to produce soups and snacks for camping. I had a legit business going for two whole days until someone broke into the store and busted everything up. I lost everything."

His heart rate increases.

Is she talking about the health food store Chris vandalized?

"Did they have insurance?"

"Yeah, but I couldn't just go out and buy all the wild stuff I lost."

"Right."

"I could've started over again, but it just hasn't felt like the right time and place to chase that dream again," she smiles at him, "It's really great what you're doing here in Rainy Bay."

He shifts uneasily in his seat.

"Wild at Hart," he says, "good name."

She laughs, "I was working on it. It always felt a little silly, slipping my name in there like that."

Finished with his supper, Niigaanii walks outside the camp and uses water from his bottle to clean his fingers.

The sun makes its way to the horizon; it'll be set in a half-hour and dark in an hour.

"It's eight-thirty now," he says, "We've got three coolers to fill by about four o'clock tomorrow. The sooner we call it a day, the sooner we can start. I'll be up early; I never miss a sunrise these days."

Winnow

Winnow listens to the songs of frogs and wonders what Niigaanii is doing in his tent.

Before she closes her eyes and drifts off to sleep, she sends a text. *Sorry Jeff, turns out I won't be available. Hope you find some good help for the restaurant.*

***

The next morning, she unzips her tent and peeks around camp. It's quiet but for the birds. She emerges with a stretch and tosses enough small sticks on the coals to fuel a French press.

She sips her coffee, studying the face of Niigaanii's tent. She checks the time on her phone, it's eight a.m.

Has he gone off already?

A rustling of his sleeping bag answers her question. A few minutes later, he pokes his head through the flap. He rubs his eyes, looking puzzled by what he sees.

"I thought you said you're always up before the sun."

He sees her and smiles and crawls out of his tent.

***

They finish their oatmeal and coffee and load their packs with containers from the coolers.

"Shall we?" he says.

"Hell yeah."

A ten-minute hike brings them to a large clearing dotted with small pines and cedars.

"Wow," she says, the lake visible way at the far end of the clearing, which is full of blueberry bushes and on closer inspection, strawberries, too.

"Okay, what's the prize? What do I get if I win?" he says.

"Huh?"

"For the competition. Everyone loves a good berry hunt."

His playfulness surprises her, but she's quick to accept his challenge, "What about this?" she says and pulls out one of her hori hori knives.

He pats his own digger hanging on his pack, "How about truth and dare? Biggest blueberry gets a truth and smallest strawberry gets a dare?"

Being the quietly competitive person she is, she tosses her good sense aside, the one that wonders, what if he asks something too personal or dares her to kiss him on the you-know-what?

"You're on," she says.

He sings as she fills her containers.

"These are some damn good blueberries," she says when he catches her stuffing several handfuls into her mouth.

She works her way to the edge of the clearing and stands on the charcoal boulders of the shore. Niigaanii's voice whirls away on the wind, leaving land behind where the calls of lake gulls pick up. Waves on rocks gently crash in, the hum of insect wings tick away the seconds, and a sapsucker knocks a wood block in the distance.

They pick for an hour and find a circular patch of springy, silky moss, about twelve feet in diameter and mostly enclosed by tiny cedars near the water's edge.

She wonders what it would feel like to lie next to him on the moss.

They pick some more and stop to sit in the shade of the largest spruce tree to compare fruit.

If I win, maybe I'll dare him to jump from the rocks into the lake butt-naked.

He lies on his back a few feet away but close enough for her to see the sky reflected in his eyes. She joins him in a supine position and is instantly pulled into the endless blue swim.

What is up, and what is down? She marvels at the bright-blue drink of space; blue-because-of-the-sun-blue or the design of the human eye or the interpretation of grey matter? The lower clouds fluff lazily by. Those inhabiting higher realms are more wisp in form, never to be grasped by hand or mind. Reflected in the movement of the retinal witness is the activation of corporeal memory of backs to earth.

If he wins, I hope he dares me to purr and roll around on that bed of moss.

He drops his arm toward her, to rest between the bristle of leaf and berry. His stained fingers open to reveal a pile of strawberries. A quick glance at his lips reveals them also coated in a red berry glaze.

She dives her fingertips into his palm to feel for a winner. The bittiest ones are wedged between his fingers, forcing her to fumble around and tickle at his flesh as she pulls them out.

"You have to eat the losers, it's a rule," he says.

One by one, she compares them with her own speck of a strawberry, eating from the cup of his flesh like he's her personal snack bowl.

"Well?" he says after she's picked his palm clean.

Her silence tells him he's won.

He turns to face her, propping himself up on his elbow, "I dare you... to," he begins, but is interrupted by a boom of lightning so loud that Winnow's skull feels like it's split in two. He grabs her hand, "Follow me."

Niigaanii

Niigaanii leads Winnow through the eye-shutting downpour. They stumble about until they reach the rocky overhang of the cave.

He lets go of her hand, "I find it a little suspicious how fast this storm arrived," he says, "Not a cloud in the sky."

She wrings her hair, "Wow."

Pictographs circle the walls of the cave. Opposite the entry, is a spiral.

"I think that's how those spirits from the little island get over here," Niigaanii says.

"A portal?"

"Something like that."

"I might as well play this now," she says and hands him a whopper of a double blueberry she kept under wraps until now, a clear winner.

"Do doubles count?"

"It wasn't in the rules."

"Well, then doubles are good for two plays; the first one is yours, and the second one is mine," he grins.

"I bet you were one of those kids who made up the rules as they go."

"My whole life. You can play your double, but first, it's still my turn."

"No, it isn't. You said, 'I dare you to follow me.' Once a dare is spoken, it can't be reversed. That's the nature of the dare."

He rubs his arms for warmth and searches for a way around her logic.

With the storm, the temperature dropped a good fifteen degrees. Winnow finds a small supply of dry branches and gets a fire going.

"Now, talk," she says.

He says the first thing that pops into his head, "Today was the first time I slept in past sunrise in a year."

That was easy, he thinks.

"Bo-ring. I need context or it doesn't count."

Shit.

Winnow stokes the little flame.

"When I left Minneapolis, my girlfriend at the time, Cindy, came back to Rainy Bay with me. She's from here. The cabin I live in now was my grandpa's. Anyway, not long after we moved in, she left one morning before I woke up. Took the van we bought together. Wouldn't return my calls. A few weeks later, I heard she was with some musician, hauling his equipment around in our van."

"So, what was it about her?"

"What do you mean?"

"What made it so hard when she left?"

After a pause, he says, "We went to high school together, graduated together. Cindy moved away after high school but came back and started working with my mom at the elementary school. They worked together for two years and became friends. My mom died just after Cindy and I started dating." Another pause, "Losing Cindy reminded me of losing my mom again." He clears his throat, "What about you, why'd you stay with your ex if he wasn't nice to you?"

"Well... when I met Chris, I wasn't attracted to him for his looks or what he does for work or anything like that. He reminded me of everyone I loved who was dealt a shitty hand. The wounded need the most love, I thought, and I wanted to love him, to help him heal. Eventually, I outgrew the ability to love and not feel loved in return."

"What made you want to be happy?"

"A lot of self-work, and then about six months ago, a couple hired me to cater their tenth-anniversary dinner with wild foods. After ten years, they were still excited to explore together. I never had that with Chris. The next day, I was out picking ode'iminan. I was crouched down with my hands under the leaves. I spaced out for a few minutes until I felt a flow of energy like the kind plants often send out when they want to speak. I looked down and, in each hand, I was holding a strawberry. They were still attached to the plant, and together, the little green stems coming off the fruits formed a heart. I got a download of information, and they told me I would witness two hearts of a bigger love if I let my current relationship go. Chris proposed a week later."

"You said yes?"

"I didn't want to argue. I was working up to leaving, and then he cheated on me and I decided I didn't owe him anything, no explanation, not one more ounce of my serenity."

Show her the jar.

He exhales and pulls out the blueberry jam pint jar that now holds maple candies.

"Zeen-zeh-baaaaa-kwaaad!" she exclaims, seeing the candies inside.

102

He chuckles and passes her the jar and sits back on his haunches, watching her closely.

"Where did you get this?"

"From you."

"When did you get this from me? The only jam that left the store was a couple for my grandma that I sent with Mel, a few I took home, and..."

"And one jar of blueberry you sold to a cook at a restaurant in Minneapolis."

Her mouth drops, "Are you serious?" she says, "I can't believe it, I knew you looked familiar."

He nods his head, "I couldn't remember where I knew you from until the other night when you had that plum jam on the beach."

"Why didn't you say something?"

He shrugs, "I wondered if you remembered."

They sit quietly, huddling on opposite sides of the little flame. He tries not to stare at her, and he can tell she's doing the same; a clump of mud becomes interesting.

Finally, she laughs.

"What?"

She covers the sides of her face with her hands, "This is embarrassing, but I remember telling Mel I sold my first jar of jam to a cute guy at a restaurant."

His skin prickles. He raises his eyes to hers, "Oh yeah?"

"Yeah," she opens the jar, "It's good to see it's still in use." She pulls out a pressed sugar leaf and holds it out.

Her fingers touch his skin as he accepts it into his palm. His heart pounds and he adjusts his sitting to hide his excitement.

Does she know what Chris did? Should I ask her?

She nibbles her sugar, "What was she like, your mom?"

"She was really funny, kind, patient. She used to say, 'There are three kinds of people in the world, Niigaanii: those who wash their hands after they wash their ass in the shower; those who don't; and those who don't wash their ass. Remember to wash your ass, son.'"

After their laughter dies down, Niigaanii asks her, "What did Shannon say to you yesterday?"

"Who?"

"The woman at the Trading Post."

"She asked if you told me about your scar."

He shakes his head, "Shannon is Cindy's cousin. We used to all hang out, but she's been weird since Cindy and I broke up, like she has to take Cindy's side even though Cindy doesn't live here anymore."

He quiets.

You don't have to say anything just because Shannon has a big mouth.

He tells her anyway.

"When I was seventeen, me, my dad, and Bibs parked at the east cliff. We'd been drinking all night. I heard my dad tell the first responders he passed out, why we went over. It was an 18-foot drop. The water wasn't deep enough to sink the car. I don't know what would've happened if it was. I hit my head pretty hard, and Bibs was asleep with her knees on the back of the seat."

"What happened to your dad?"

"Didn't see much of him after that. I've been sober since, so our lifestyles don't mesh. It was hard getting sober, with all my friends drinking."

"I bet. I was sixteen when I knew I needed to quit. I tried several times; I'd be sober for a few months but it didn't stick until I was twenty-nine."

"How old are you now?"

"Thirty-three. You?"

104

"Thirty-seven."

The pounding water eases into a soft rain.

Niigaanii looks outside, "We should get back to camp and ride out the storm."

Winnow

"**M**y tent's gone," Niigaanii says.

"What do you mean it's gone?"

They squint through the rain. Not one stake lies where it had been.

"Come on," she says through the downpour, taking the lead and pulling on his sleeve, indicating he follow her into her tent.

It's an hour from dusk but the sky is dark and the tent is dimly lit. Their cold bodies force grunts and the occasional swear word as they peel off wet clothes down to their underwear.

Thuck! His pants land in a wet heap in a corner near the door. He sits on the bed in his wet boxers, the color of the material is lighter than the skin of his legs, which he hugs into himself. He lets go to blow hot air into his hands.

She digs in a pile of blankets and pulls out a beach and hand towel. She tosses him the beach towel and uses the smaller one to dry her face and hair.

"Scientific research shows the big spoon gets more heat to their core than the little spoon," he says and wraps the larger towel around her after a quick dab of his skin.

"Big spoon?"

"Yup," he says, crawling across the air mattress and edging himself near the wall of the tent to make room for her, the big spoon.

She laughs, "Scientific research, huh?"

"Should only take fifteen, twenty minutes to put the pink back in your lips." He pats the mattress behind him, "I'll tell you a story."

A sharp chill bites at her hardened nipples and she squirms to lay behind him, keeping a small distance between their bodies. It's the first time she smells his skin wet; he's river stones and green manoomin. Excitement plumps her veins, causing certain parts of her to be aware of the distance to cross in order to reach him. It takes all her willpower to not wrap her leg around him and suggest they warm up by doing more than spooning.

Her teeth chatter through a forced exhale as she pulls the pile of blankets on top of them.

Before she asks if it's okay to put her freezing fingers on him, he says, "You've got to get closer than that if you want this to work."

Does he mean physically or emotionally?

She wriggles her body to fit snugly against his.

Can he feel my nipples?

Her bare stomach kisses the smooth skin of his lower back, her pubic area and the top of her thighs forming a perfect cup to shape around his buttocks, the shape of which is unmistakable beneath his damp boxers.

This is perfectly okay. We are professionals who just happen to be counting on the heat of the other to not freeze.

She presses the side of her face to cover the goosebumps on his neck and slides her hand unconfidently up to his waist.

He lifts his arm so she can stick her hand through. He grabs it and guides it to lay on his chest, where he covers her arm and hand with his. His hand is larger than hers, and although she can feel callouses, he holds hers gently.

The skin on his chest is soft and his muscles are firm. She must control herself to not move her hand around and feel him. Her shins nestle into the backs of his calves, and he lifts a leg to let her slip a foot between his.

Is this more than a kind gesture on his part, to warm me? Does this mean anything more for him?

When they reach maximum cuddle status, she feels more comfortable than she ever remembers being and falls asleep while he tells her a story about the sugarbush.

Within moments of crossing the threshold from wake to dream, she grows tall through the years, sees the forest change, feels the sway of the breeze, the hot of many summers' heat, the thrashing of storms, and then time settles on an early spring morning, and Niigaanii is caressing her bark. He produces his tap and gently presses it into her. He holds onto her truck and laps at her sap, which trickles freely. Sounds of pleasure emanate from him as he quenches his thirst.

She wakes, her face close to his. He sleeps soundly, his hand resting on her side. She can feel him on her thigh and doesn't push him off but rather closes her eyes and basks in his warmth. A few minutes go by before he wakes. He pulls away and removes his hand to his own side.

Soon she can see the whites of his eyes, "I had the loveliest dream of being in the sugarbush," she says, blushing in the still-dark tent, "You were there."

"Oh?"

She envisions him gleefully drinking her sap and wonders what might become of the moment were she to reveal such an intimate detail to him now.

She chickens out, "You were gathering sap."

Silence sits in the darkness between their ears. He doesn't offer what he'd dreamt that had made him lean hard into her.

"Hold still," she says and tickles his ear. Goosebumps form on his arm; the shape and color of his shoulder, the lines of his jaw, and his lips, distract her from the arachnid on his ear, "Where did it go?" she says.

"Where'd what go?"

"The tick."

He laughs, "Tick hunter!"

As her fingertips search his neck, the hungry ache to be with a man is fed a little. She's had a taste.

"Aha!" She slips out of the blankets and tosses the tick out through the zipper.

As she goes to get back under the blankets with him, she stops to wonder if the reason has changed. She is dry. She is warm. Why is she getting into the same blanket as this man? If she gets back in without question, without putting any meaning into the why, what will happen? Would they have sex? Is that what she wants? Maybe she's overthinking things. In an effort to cultivate the good she's found in his company, she fumbles around for something to cover herself with. She pulls on a t-shirt and then drops to her knees by him.

"I guess being the big spoon does work." She tugs on one of the blankets, "Now scootch over," she says and laughs as he unrolls from the blanket like a burrito spilling its contents.

***

After another hour of hard sleep, they pack up and quietly make their way to the beach, stopping to gather chanterelles and wild greens along the way.

When they get to the bay, the buzzing in Winnow's pocket informs her of the first signal she's had in two days.

"Jeez, what ya got in there?" Niigaanii says.

She laughs, "Pfft, yeah right."

Now, if Mel's pocket was vibrating, that might be a different story.

He perks up, remembering something, "Hey, can I borrow that?"

"My dildo?"

"Shit," he laughs.

She hands him the phone.

"Miigwech. I was supposed to get ahold of Bruce last night about the wrap design for The Harvester."

Winnow loads the canoe and climbs into the back.

He returns from his walk down the beach and pushes on the nose of the canoe. He hops in, "I called Bibs, the boys don't have covid." He hands her the phone, "I, uh, opened a text when I was trying to close a call. It might've been important."

Winnow

After spending the last two days relaxing in Niigaanii's company, the trip back to town was the most awkward hour of her life, because the text Niigaanii intercepted was from Jeff.

Cum give me a hand when you can, Jeff's text read.

Does Niigaanii think she wants to give Jeff a "hand"? Because she doesn't. But she can't tell Niigaanii that. She can't say, "I was toying with the idea of having revenge sex until you came along," because what the hell does that mean?

Jeff never received the text Winnow sent earlier telling him she was passing on the job. She expected it to go through before now but instead, it had vanished.

Piece of shit phone.

The festival is in full swing upon their return into town and the transformation is a welcome distraction. The fundraiser for NeeJee's SkweeJees is in full swing in the parking lot of the Trading Post. Tents are up and people from many Indigenous nations buzz the festival grounds, walking between the hotel, garden, beach, and canopies for fish smoking, acorn flour making, vegetable canning and more. Others play horseshoes, basketball, or lacrosse. There's corn husk doll making, art and dry goods vendors, live music, caravans traveling to and from local food production sites, and the sound of a drum group practicing songs at one of the campsites fills the air.

"I'll drop you and the coolers in the kitchen before I go home to clean up," Niigaanii says.

They make three trips to carry their bounty to the walk-in cooler and as they do so, Winnow can't help but think that the best thing she found on the island wasn't physical food at all, but a growing, healthy desire for this man.

Winnow accompanies Niigaanii once more to his truck to get her backpack.

"I'll be back soon," he says.

Walking into the building, Winnow holds the door for an elder in a red baseball cap with an assortment of military patches and a feather hanging in the back.

"Ol' Gusty!" The man says, seeing Dusty at his desk.

"Heh, heh, heh," Dusty chuckles.

"Gusty?" Winnow says to the man in the red cap.

"This guy could clear a room when we were kids," the elder replies.

"Chi-jaanzh," Dusty says, "been a while."

The man looks at Winnow, "He says I have a big nose, but what he means is I have a big, owahiya!" he says and rubs his elbow.

"Oh shush!" A woman comes in behind him, hitting him on the elbow, "Take my bag eh, big nose." She chuckles.

"Yes, dear," the man says, grinning. He looks at Dusty, "They keep you out here by the door to air you out?"

Dusty chuckles and the man pats him on the shoulder before walking past.

112

***

Winnow gets to her room. The MMA fighter's backpack is on the sofa, and her toothbrush is in the bathroom but she's not there.

Winnow's pocket vibrates.

It's a text from Chris. *Miss you, babe. I'll be there soon.*

Winnow's stomach churns.

On her way down to the kitchen, Melanie calls.

"Chris said he'll be here soon."

"What the fuck! Win, I know you planned to ignore him but you're gonna have to tell him to fuck off."

"I know, I know, I will. Hey, what if I dye my hair blonde and when he comes and sees that I obviously got the texts, I kick him right in the balls and ask him if he still likes blondes best?"

"Dude, that's both hilarious and makes me worry about you. You need to get on this, like right now, before he gets there."

Niigaanii

Niigaanii arrives at his cabin to find Mr. Puppers napping in the sun on the porch. Seeing the pup sets him at ease.

Mr. Puppers flips his head up to catch the intruder of his nap. To Niigaanii's surprise, the dog lays his head back down and resumes his comfort.

Wanting to relish in the moment of the pup's growing trust in him, he sits on the bottom stoop.

"Can I tell you something?"

Mr. Puppers takes a stiff, four-legged stretch, his paws extending out over the top step.

"I always told people Cindy left because she thought I vandalized that store."

The dog lifts an eyelid.

"I think I need to tell this woman I like, Winnow, the real reason she left."

A snort.

"What's she gonna think of me?"

***

Back at the hotel, Niigaanii works the check-in counter so Bibs could step away. He hasn't made it back to the kitchen yet, back to her, Winnow. He wishes they could have more time alone together, but he's having doubts, given the flirtatious messages from that guy Jeff.

Pfft, Jeff. That guy sounds like a joke.

He turns to the bellhop girl next to the counter and smiles, "I don't know if there's anything that could break the good mood I'm in."

The girl smiles.

If it weren't for the lack of a neck tattoo of a big-breasted she-devil holding a hot iron, Niigaanii would swear the man walking towards the check-in counter was none other than Winnow's ex-fiance, Chris Brown. The man is a Native dude with the same undercut and top slicked to the side as Chris, but this guy has on matte brown oxfords and green khakis instead of basketball shoes and oversized jeans.

Holy shit, it's him.

Not knowing what else to say, Niigaanii chokes out a "Hey."

"Sup?" Chris says, absorbed in his phone.

A twenty-something blonde hovers at Chris' elbow. She wears short white shorts and a mostly unbuttoned top through which her bosom breathes anxiously as if she's expecting to be ambushed at any moment.

This must be Emily.

Just then, Dusty storms up the hallway, a look of thunder across his brow. He's cradling his coffee mug, which is in pieces.

"What happened to your mug?" Niigaanii asks.

A few drips of coffee trickle down Dusty's fingers. He looks at Chris and mumbles something about not using his nightstick once on the job in twenty years and disappears around the corner towards the maintenance room.

Chris looks up from his phone at Niigaanii now but doesn't seem to register that they know one another, "I'm looking for my fiancé," he says.

Emily rolls her eyes.

Niigaanii stays quiet.

"Her name is Winnow Hart. Can you tell me what room she's in?"

This motherfucker seriously gonna stand here and act like he doesn't know who the fuck I am?

"I can't give out guest information, but you're welcome to wait in the lobby while I call her room," Niigaanii says.

"Sure," Chris says and turns to Emily, "You might as well find a room. I'm gonna stay a night or two." He walks across the lobby and sits down in a chair by the windows.

"Hi, can I get a room?" Emily says.

"Hello," Niigaanii says, trying to keep the boil in his blood from steaming out of his ears, "I'm sorry, we're fully booked through Sunday."

"You've got nothing? Can you check?"

"We've been booked weeks out due to the festival. There's free camping on the grounds, if that works for you."

"I've never been camping. I don't have a tent."

Well, I'm sure as hell not telling you about the lenders.

"Don't we still have a few tents for occasions like this?" Bibs says, coming up from the other end of the counter, grabbing a sheet of paper, and walking back down the hall.

Thanks, sis.

116

Niigaanii suppresses his annoyance, "I can see if we have a spare in the back if you're interested."

"Uhm, let me get back to you about that," she says and clicks her way over to Chris, "Can you help me set up a tent?" she asks him.

Niigaanii dials Winnow's room on the desk phone and is relieved when she doesn't pick up, "She didn't answer. We can try again in a bit," he says across the lobby to Chris.

"I gotta run out to the car," Chris tells Emily.

Emily pouts her way back to the desk, "I'll take one of those tents you mentioned."

Just then, Raquel bounces around the corner, "Sup, Boo?" she says, scrunching her face and lifting her lips in a fanged, teasing smile.

"Are you going to help me set it up?" Emily asks Niigaanii. She leans across the counter to expose more of her bosom.

"Set what up?" Raquel says.

"Our guest wants to camp and needs a tent," he says to Raquel.

Raquel looks at Emily draped towards Niigaanii and says, "I got this Boo."

Niigaanii tilts his head back and tries to physically wipe the frustration from his face.

To the woman, Raquel says, "Come on, I'll show you where the tents are. I'll even help you set it up in a nice shady spot on the west lot by the trees."

"You're going to set it up for her?" Niigaanii says to Raquel.

Raquel leads the woman towards the storeroom, "I think you mean, thank you, Raquel."

"Thank you, Raquel."

A minute later, Winnow walks through the lobby.

"Hey," she says to Niigaanii.

"Hey," he says, "your fiancé is here."

She gives him a "what the fuck" look, "He's not my fiancé."

"He thinks he is."

"Is he staying here?"

"If he camps, I suppose."

"Did you tell him what room I'm in?"

"No, but if you wanna hang around, he'll be back any minute and you can tell him then if you like."

Why did you say that?

Winnow moves quickly down the hall.

How could this get any worse?

"Hey Niigaanii, how're you doing?"

Oh, no.

"Cindy," he says and turns to see her familiar high ponytail of long brown hair, the ends falling around the middle of her back. She wears a flowy, light-colored dress with flowers.

He shrugs his shoulders, "Working a lot. Doing great, actually."

"Oh? You get that food truck going?"

How does she know about The Harvester?

"Yep. What about you?"

She smiles, "I'm good." She rubs her belly, which has a slight bump, "I'm pregnant."

Don't ask who the dad is. Don't ask who the dad is.

"Who's the dad?"

"His name's Lyle," Cindy says, motioning to a man in a cowboy hat and boots standing across the lobby, "We met in Santa Fe."

Upon further inspection, Niigaanii notices she's wearing a wedding band.

"Congratulations."

"Thanks."

Niigaanii purses his lips and nods his head. He hadn't met anyone after Cindy, until this week.

"I met someone too," he says, surprising himself, "We actually met a long time ago, back in The Cities."

"I'm happy for you," she smiles, "Well, it was nice seeing you. Take care of yourself," Cindy says and joins her husband. She hadn't said anything about their breakup, and there was no apology, but when she said she was happy for him, he believed her.

It was time for him to move forward and embrace his new happy.

Winnow

Niigaanii enters the kitchen, "Good to see you two back," he says to Derek and Michael, finding them cleaning berries at the sink.

"When's Raquel coming?" Derek says.

"Who wants to know?" Raquel says, coming in behind Niigaanii.

Derek blushes, "Sup?"

Winnow goes to the walk-in cooler and looks over the accumulated ingredients for the next day's dinner.

Niigaanii follows her in, "How're we doing?"

We as in the food or we as in us?

"We have a lot of walleye just brought in that still need to be filleted, also venison, lots of fresh veggies, and the berries, mushrooms, and wild greens from the island."

"You wanna put a menu and prep list together?" he says and holds up a marker.

***

Several minutes later, Winnow carries a whiteboard into the kitchen, prompting oohs and aahs over the menu:

Mains:

Acorn and manoomin flour crusted walleye/roasted venison/ or roasted wild mushroom sandwich

Fruit sauces to pair with mains:

blueberry bergamot (venison), hot pepper plum (walleye/mushroom)

Sides:

Wild greens and berry salad with creamy nettle dressing

Roasted veg and hominy salad

Raw veggies with wild spinach and leek dip

Sweets:

Frozen manoomin custard with hazelnut butter caramel and candied berries

Wild jam and nut butter pinwheels

Beverages:

Wild sodas

blueberry

strawberry

raspberry

grape

Wintergreen tea

Coffee

***

Winnow walks around the kitchen, observing hands and spirits working with wild ingredients; people smiling and laughing, all receiving a great, nourishing charge of love from the spirits of the earth. It's impossible to stay upset in the presence of this love.

She stops by Niigaanii, who's cleaning chanterelles in preparation for roasting.

"How're we doing?" she asks him.

He smiles and moves down the counter, making room for her.

After they clean the mushrooms, Winnow gives a demo to the volunteers on how to make manoomin flour.

"Manoomin flour should be silky between the fingertips," she says.

She pulls a tablespoon of the powder from the blender and dips her middle finger into it. She rubs it to the tip of her thumb and discovers a new memory connected to this sensation; the silkiness of Niigaanii's skin. A shiver runs down her spine and anchors in her loins.

"Like a silky patch of moss you could lounge around on all day," Niigaanii says. He blushes but keeps his eyes on the dehydrator racks nearby, where he tends to sheets of half-dry, slightly sweet hazelnut butter. He spreads thick berry sauce on top and returns them to the dehydrator. Later, they will be glazed with honey, rolled, topped with roasted nuts, and sliced into pinwheels.

Winnow turns the blender on high to distract from her own cheeky redness.

Bibs comes in, "There's a bear hanging around west of the festival grounds. Everyone, please help make sure food and scraps aren't left out. Let's not add to the compost until the festival is over."

"We can put the fish guts in the freezer until then," Niigaanii says.

"I wish someone would throw those fish guts in Chris' tent," Winnow says quietly to no one in particular.

Niigaanii

F riday morning arrives and Niigaanii carries his slightly-too-big ribbon shirt down the hall and knocks on the door. He knocks louder.

The door opens. It's Raquel, "I didn't hear you knocking, I was in the bathroom."

"Musta been a bunch of loud noises in there, eh?"

Raquel rolls her eyes, "Ew. Well, come in." She opens the door wider and pulls him through.

Fabrics of all colors lie strewn about.

"What's going on in here?"

"We talked about this," she gives him a look, "in your truck, on our date, if anyone would even call it that."

"Oh, right. You're... on a quilting retreat?"

"I'm impressed you were listening. I was lying about that, though, I'm just here until I can move to the dorms in St. Cloud next month. My mom doesn't want me at home right now."

She grabs a measuring tape from one of the many craft boxes lining the walls.

"Okay, now don't freak out on me, I gotta get close to get the measurements."

"I'm not going to freak out," he says, "I've been touched by women before."

"Well, you're awfully squirrelly."

"Nothing wrong with a squirrel hiding his nuts. There's always crows and cougars and such trying to steal them."

"Pfft. She leans in close, "How'd you get this scar?"

"Car accident." The ease at which he answers this question surprises him.

She kneels in front of him.

He takes a step back, "What are you doing?"

"I've got a surprise for you."

"A surprise?"

She puts a hand on her hip, "Not that kind of surprise. I know you like that cook and I'm over it. Are you going to let me help you or not?"

He clears his throat but keeps an eye on her as she measures his waist and inseam, "I know your mom," he says, "she went to school with my cousin Jay. I don't talk to her much these days now that she's tribal chairwoman, but I know her well enough to know she's not trying to get rid of you. All kids butt heads with their parents now and again. She has that new boyfriend, what's his name?" Niigaanii asks, despite knowing his name.

"Justin," Raquel says with resentment.

"Does he have kids?"

"Two little jerks. One moved into my room." She stands up, "I knew they'd fit you perfectly!" she says and retrieves a pair of black embroidered jeans from a dresser.

"Those are awesome. How much?"

"They're for you, take them," she holds them out.

"I insist. I know what it's like to not get paid enough for your work."

"Fine."

He takes out his wallet and pulls out three twenties and looks at her.

She motions her hands as if to say, "Keep going".

He chuckles and gives her a hundred-dollar bill.

"Wow, thanks!" she says, "I'll have your shirt fixed in just a minute if you want to wait," she says and takes his ribbon shirt to her sewing machine.

He sits down on the edge of the bed behind her.

"Did you get along with your parents?" she asks.

"My mom, yes. My dad, not so much."

"Why not?" she asks, popping in a bobbin.

He thinks for a minute and remembers how Winnow described Chris, "Do you know anyone who does messed-up shit just because?"

"More than a few."

"That was my dad."

She turns around to see him motion to his scar.

"Your dad did that to you?"

He nods, "That's how I know your mom isn't trying to get rid of you. She's not like my dad. She cares what happens to you." He clears his voice, "And you're nice to have around."

Raquel raises an eyebrow and laughs, "Shut up." She turns back to the machine.

"You're like the talented, ambitious little cousin I never had."

"Right," she laughs, "And you're kind of cool for an old guy."

He chuckles.

That's more like it.

"I'm actually seeing someone now."

"Oh?"

"It's Derek."

"That's great."

"Done," Raquel says, trimming a thread. She hands the shirt to him, "Try it on."

He slips it on over his t-shirt, "It fits great, miigwech." He stands up, "I really should get back to the kitchen. I'm waiting to hear if The Harvester is ready to get picked up today."

Niigaanii leaves Raquel's room and walks down the hall. Before he gets to the turn for the elevator by Winnow's room, he hears voices around the hall.

"Are you kidding me, Emily?" Chris says in a hushed voice.

"I thought you wanted this. I thought you wanted me."

"You've maybe ruined my life and you're telling me you did it on purpose? Fuck, Emily. You know you shouldn't even be here, right?"

"Winnow and I are friends, I can support a friend, can't I?" Emily says in a sickly-sweet voice, "Besides, I think she got the pictures and doesn't care. That's good, right?"

"Shh! Keep your voice down."

"Whatever, Chris. I'll be outside."

The elevator door closes, and one set of feet continues down the hall.

"Open up, I hear you in there!" Chris says, pounding on the door to Winnow's room.

Niigaanii approaches him and says, "Chris?"

Chris looks annoyed, "Do I know you?" He turns back to the door and pounds louder.

The door opens a crack and Chris sticks his arm in. And then he stumbles backward down the hall and crashes into a garbage bin.

Winnow

L eaving her room for the kitchen, Winnow hears voices down the hall. She stops to see Raquel put her hands on Niigaanii and pull him into her room.

Winnow fumbles to get back into her room. Once inside, she sinks to the floor. Her chest empties of air as she lets the weight of the possibilities sit on top of her. She picks up her phone and looks at the photos of Chris and Emily for the first time in days.

"Why? Why does it always end like this? Whether four years or four days, I always feel like a fool."

She texts Melanie. *Maybe I should dye my hair blonde. And instead of wanting to kick men in the balls, I'll offer to lick more of them. Would that help? I don't fucking know.* She deletes the text without sending it.

She opens her conversation with Jeff.

At least he flirts with everyone, so I know what I'd be getting into, she thinks.

128

She reads the last of their conversation. Her heart shifts around in her chest, threatening to shift Niigaanii right out of the spot he positioned himself into.

Jeff's last response was, *Cum give me a hand when you can.*

What had Niigaanii thought when he read it?

Maybe I've got their relationship all wrong. Or maybe he just got sucked into Raquel's room for a quickie.

She dries her eyes and leaves the room, determined to do the job she was hired to do.

***

"Tables, food warmers, carafes; everything is almost set up. I can't believe how smooth everything is running," Winnow says to Bibs as they arrange napkins and silverware on a table in the large dining hall. "This has been the most hassle-free gig I've ever worked."

Except for that brother of yours, Winnow thinks as Niigaanii enters the hall wearing a ribbon shirt and fancy pants; his hair braided.

"Everyone out of the hall!" Harvey shouts.

"What?" Winnow and Bibs say in unison before turning to see water running across the carpet.

"A pipe burst, we have to shut everything down," Harvey says.

Winnow follows Niigaanii down the hall, the smell of him she still finds reassuring and welcome in her nose.

They enter the kitchen just as the power goes out.

"What are we going to do? We're supposed to feed hundreds of people in two hours!" Delores says to an army of volunteers.

"It's a good thing you have all those windows for light," Winnow says, "And most everything is cooked, it just needs to be reheated and served. We can't use the stovetops or ovens. And we can't serve in the hall. What else do we have?"

"About a dozen large iron kettles," Niigaanii says, "We don't have power or water, but we always have fire. We can set the kettles up outside the window," He points to the one with no screen, "and run water from the garden. It's across the field but Susie and Viola keep enough hose to water the moon."

"Yes!" Delores says, "We can still use the kitchen for prep, but everyone should start using more gloves since we can't wash our hands just yet. I'll get more from the storage room."

"We need to rethink the menu," Winnow says to the group.

"Let's just make soup," Michael says.

"He's right," Niigaanii seconds the idea, "we need to simplify. How about two kettles of walleye, two of deer, and two vegetarian? That should be plenty of food."

"Oh, you good boy!" Delores says, back already with a stack of glove boxes, "The vegetables are roasted, and we still have time to cook the manoomin in the kettles."

"It's half-cooked now," Derek says, standing next to a giant pot of wild rice.

"We have all of this great batter for cornbread buns but nowhere to cook it with the ovens down," Winnow says, "It would be nice if we had some sort of bread."

"What about Buns by Bev?" Raquel says, entering the kitchen and pulling on an apron.

Oh, great.

"Yes, Buns by Bev! I'll get her on the phone, back in a minute," Delores says and scurries out of the kitchen again.

"Derek, Michael," Niigaanii says, "you two take some of the volunteers to get the water going."

Derek looks across the room to Raquel and smiles but nods at several of the helpers standing near him, indicating they follow. The brothers lead the group at a near sprint from the kitchen.

"I'll find Harvey and get the kettles, but I'll need help," Niigaanii says.

"Take the rest of the volunteers," Delores says, "Us three will prepare the meats and vegetables for soups." Delores motions to Raquel and Winnow.

Oh, great.

***

"Doesn't he look nice in his ribbon shirt?" Raquel says once they're alone.

Winnow scrunches her eyebrows.

"He had me fix it you know, his shirt," Raquel.

"I saw you fixing him up this morning in your room," Winnow says.

Raquel stops piling roasted vegetables into a food pan, "That man wouldn't let me touch him with a ten-foot pole. And you come along and he's all ooey-gooey over you and I help him look good for you and you're gonna come at me like that?"

The lava in Winnow's veins cools, "So you two didn't...?"

Raquel laughs, "No, and I got a new boo, Derek. We hung out all night last night. But what's with that ex of *yours*? He's been stinking up the vibe around here, and that woman he's with... ish."

"They're sleeping together," Winnow says.

Raquel's eyes bulge, "Those bitches! I heard a bear tried to get into their tent last night," she says and grins, "Seems someone put fish guts under it."

Winnow laughs, "What? Was it you?"

Raquel shrugs and answers Winnow's question with a question, "Why are they here, anyway?"

Winnow shares everything with Raquel while they assemble the contents for the kettles and after mentioning the pictures Emily sent, Raquel wants to see them.

Winnow pulls out her phone but the desire to get back at Chris is gone. The whole thing just feels icky, and she realizes she's finally, completely done with it, "You know, I've been meaning to delete this garbage," she says and deletes everything and blocks their numbers. "Hey, Raquel, I'm sorry for what I said, you know, being judgy."

"That's nothing compared to my mom."

"Where is your mom?"

"At home, a couple of miles from here," Raquel looks at the clock and frowns, "for about another six hours, then she's off to D.C. for a month. I'm moving to St. Cloud for college soon, so I probably won't see her for a while."

Winnow sticks her hands into her apron pockets and feels the key-chain Bibs gave her. She pulls it out and says, "Ever ride on a scooter?"

***

After delivering a sobbing Raquel into her mother's arms, Winnow wafts bright vapors of wintergreen and mint with the lid of a pot that hangs over a fire behind the hotel. She ingests the aroma first with her nose, and then with the entirety of her being, her consciousness travels the vapor like a canoe, basting in the flow of non-localized flavor and time. Her mind, spirit, and flesh are ripe for the picking when Niigaanii approaches her.

He tilts his head up to take a whiff. Hauling heavy iron kettles and
lighting the fires had created a mess of his hair. She remembers the first
time she saw him in the kitchen, how she wanted to reach for a bit of
blueberry leaf stuck in his locks. Now, she doesn't hesitate and leans
in to remove a piece of bark with her free hand while avoiding his eyes.
She doesn't know how tell him how she wants every bit of him.

"Hey," he says quietly, "I have to tell you something."

"What is it?"

"It was Chris who vandalized the kitchen and all your stuff."

"What?"

"I hope this doesn't sound awful, but I'm glad in a way that he did,
because we might not be here, now, together. I'd probably still be with
Cindy, and you might still be with Chris. This," he holds up the little
jar he'd carried around for a year, "this brought me home. You brought
me home."

She takes a step back.

She always thought it might have been Chris that did it, but she
pushed it to the back of her mind, along with all the other reasons she
should abandon the relationship.

"How do you know it was him?"

"It's a long story, and I didn't know if I should be the one to say
anything, but after I realized how I felt about... everything, I'm sorry I
didn't tell you sooner. You're good for me, Winnow. I hope you'll let
me know if I'm good for you, too."

"You knew this whole time?"

He looks down into the kettle and nods.

The lights and sounds of the festival garble and waver around her as
humiliation strikes; what Chris did to her was the lowest point of her
self-sabotage and Niigaanii knew about it the whole time.

It was Chris.

An angry fire rages, burning up any leftover fear of confronting Chris about his bullshit.

"Winnow, I…"

He can't finish. She brushes past him, and yet the smell of him, that of boiling manoomin and burning sweet grass, sears the tinder of her heart and she wants to throw every ounce of it onto that good flame. She wants him more than anything.

***

With no running water in the bathrooms, Winnow makes a visit to a porta potty on the festival grounds. She's hovering over the seat when a familiar voice outside makes her freeze, mid-wipe.

"I'm saying our fling was a result of pent-up sexual frustration from three months of not getting any."

"You weren't getting any from Winnow because she was the one having an affair, Chris. Don't be stupid."

Winnow slumps against the wall of the porta-john.

Chris wasn't cheating on me before I stopped having sex with him.

"You're just out of sorts right now because of that bear."

"You're fucking right I am! And if I find out who put those fish guts under the tent, I swear to god."

"So that's all this is to you, then, a fling?" Emily's voice trembles, "Do you still love her?"

"Of course, I do."

Winnow, now standing on the seat, looks down through the ventilation slits to see Emily looking defeated, her head lowered.

She wipes wetness from her eyes, "Okay," Emily says. She nods her head slowly, "I'll see you around." She walks away from Chris, cutting through a line of kids waiting for a wild berry snow cone.

Just then, Winnow slips on a rogue piece of toilet paper, bounces off the side of the porta-can, and scrambles like a rat to not fall in. Upon regaining her footing, she sees Chris standing nearby looking at his phone.

"I don't love you, Chris," she says loudly through the slots. The words surprise her.

I'm so brave! she thinks and then covers a laugh. *I'm hiding in a shitter.*

A pause.

"Winnow?"

Chris bangs on the first porta-john in the lineup and makes his way down the row, "Winnow!"

The hollering from the people in the toilets doesn't stop him.

"Go home, Chris!"

Chris is at her john when Dusty appears, pointing his nightstick towards the hotel.

"Move," Dusty says.

Chris does as he's told but shouts, "I'm not leaving until I talk to you, Winnow!"

Niigaanii

The water is back on in the kitchen, thanks to a series of hoses running from the garden. Niigaanii waits outside the kitchen door for Winnow, who washes her hands inside at the sink.

She emerges.

"Can I talk to you?" Niigaanii says.

She stops.

He grabs her hands, and she doesn't pull away.

"There's something I've never told anyone. I'd like to tell you," he says.

Electricity surges from their touch and there's a promise of a beautiful life in the spark.

"My dad lied."

"What do you mean?"

"He drove us over the cliff on purpose. I saw him do it, but I couldn't stop him. I never told Bibs. I just told her I never wanted us to see him anymore."

As he speaks his truth out loud, his eyes moisten but he doesn't look away from her.

Her eyes become wet as well and she rubs his hand.

"Bibs wasn't even drinking; she was along to make sure we weren't getting into trouble. I should have protected her, but I was busy getting wasted." He wipes a tear.

"That was your dad's job, you were just a kid."

He nods, "I was angry he hurt my sister and ashamed of what he did, as our father. I was more ashamed that I still loved him. I protected him so he wouldn't go to prison. And Cindy, she didn't leave because she thought I vandalized the store. She left because I didn't turn Chris in; I didn't hold him accountable even though his actions disrupted our lives. I never told Cindy what my dad did because it felt like telling my mom. I never wanted my mother to feel worse about it than she already did, thinking it was an accident. And I'm sorry I didn't tell you I knew about Chris sooner."

Winnow nods and looks in thought, "There's never a good time to say something like that. Or to tell someone it's kinda your fault they got arrested."

"What?"

"Remember how I said I told Melanie I sold a jar of jam to a cute guy? Chris overheard me and we got into an argument, and he left. I didn't know where he went or what he was doing. I had a feeling something was wrong, but then the police had a lead, and it wasn't Chris. You didn't know me at all that day you bought my jam, but you supported my dreams more than Chris ever did. And I'm sorry for what happened to you because of it."

"I'm glad it happened," he says and pulls her hand closer toward him, "I wondered what the connection was, but it's not your fault he's a moo jiid."

Winnow laughs, "I haven't heard that in a while."

"I'm bringing it back. Oh! I almost forgot to tell you. I just saw that moo jiid get the shit kicked out of him."

"What!"

"He was trying to push his way into your room and got his ass sent across the hall by that MMA fighter."

"That's... crazy... awesome!"

A moment of silence is broken by Niigaanii's laugh.

"What?" Winnow says.

"You thought I was cute."

"Did, do. What of it?" she smiles.

It's now that Niigaanii realizes there's nothing in the way of experiencing her, if she'll have him. A longing to discover what life in her company could be like, fills him with a freedom of emotion and hope, so much so that his head feels like it just might float away from his shoulders.

He spends an amplified moment looking into her eyes and moves a little closer to her. He is about to speak when the kitchen door flings open.

It's Delores, "Oh, there you are."

"Hey, I have to go do something really quick," Niigaanii says, "I'll be back soon."

Winnow

After a whirlwind of an hour of outdoor meal service and talking to people from all over the country about the food, Winnow heads for the kitchen.

"Have you seen Niigaanii?" she asks Bibs, who's chatting in the hall with a couple of townsfolk interested in starting garden plots.

Bibs checks her watch, "He should be back any minute with The Harvester."

Winnow gets to the kitchen where Delores is showing Michael how to use the dishwasher while a few others help clean up.

Niigaanii appears at the window and Winnow realizes she's never been more excited to see anyone.

"Can you meet me out front?" He says to her as she approaches the window, "I want to show you something,"

"Will you be okay without me?" she asks Delores.

"You better go see what he's got," Delores says.

Winnow unties her apron and hangs it on the rack by the kitchen door and heads down the hall. Pushing through the front doors, the aura of the day feels extra radiant. There's a marvelous amplifying of energy at this type of event. As the people and the land wind around each other more closely in relationships, the collective energy glows more brightly, like the way sweetgrass is transformed with prayer and fire when braided.

She hears the motor of The Harvester as it slows down to give room for festivalgoers. It stops at the end of the portico where its growl is silenced.

Winnow walks out to meet Niigaanii. He's still in his ribbon shirt, only the top two buttons are undone now, revealing the neck of a t-shirt. She would like nothing more than to unbutton it the rest of the way for him and pull his t-shirt off over his head.

He looks nervous but excited.

"What do you think?" he asks, motioning to the truck that's now wrapped in green and looking like one of those big trucks that battle each other.

"It's...awesome."

"There's something else new, too," he holds out his hand and she takes it.

Her cheeks pinch into a wheel of cheese. She takes his hand and floats behind him up the steps of the truck.

He walks her to a counter where a paper box sits. A half dozen smaller boxes sit next to it.

"Change is about maintaining a new momentum into the future, and this," he motions between them and moves closer to her, "is the most natural movement in my entire life."

She understands him with every part of her; her every cell singing to move in his direction.

His anticipation is too much, "Here," he says as if he'd expected her to rip into it the moment she saw the box. He undoes the top flap and leaves the rest to her.

Inside is a jar of jam. Not just any jam but made from the little wild strawberries they picked together during their time on the island.

"Is this from what we harvested?"

"En'."

Not only did Niigaanii make a batch of jam, but he designed a label.

"Native Love Jams," Winnow says, her eyes and other unseen parts of her, moisten with approval.

He points to the jar, "Moozoons is on standby for the go-ahead to make the design legit."

She looks at him, "The go-ahead?"

He pulls a stool out from under the counter and sits down, "What do you think?" He pulls her close, wedging her into the warmth of his open legs, "Is what we have here legit?" He nods to the design, but she knows what he's really talking about.

"Oh, shitchyeah it is," she says, and wraps her arms around his neck, his hair silky soft under her wrists. She pecks at his lips, and the hair on her body stands on end.

He pushes his tongue against her mouth, and she opens to his exploration.

She pulls away to say, "We should probably see if we're needed in the kitchen, right?"

He cups his hands to her buttocks and pulls her closer, the heat smoldering between her thighs.

He smiles, "Probably."

Niigaanii

They walk around the side of the building to use the door designated for staff while the water mess is drying.

Niigaanii is about to pull it open when Delores beats him to it.

She pops her head out, "What do you want?" Delores says and gives them a playful side-eye, "The kitchen is full, so don't bother trying to get in here."

"Well, what the hell are we supposed to do?" Niigaanii chuckles.

"I'm sure you'll think of something," Delores says, then lets the door close between them, and then quickly pops out again, "I'm getting paid at the manager rate today, right?"

"Shitchyeah, you are!" Niigaanii says.

Delores disappears.

The side of the building is quieter than the main festival area, with just a few people walking through, grasshoppers snapping lazily at them as they pass.

"Now you just need a crew for The Harvester," Winnow says, leaning a shoulder on the building.

"You're right," he says, a dopey smile all for her, "What do you say?"

"What do you mean?"

He props himself next to her, "You've kind of been interviewing all week. With Michael starting as the new dishwasher and Derek off to St. Cloud next month, I could use the help."

"Derek's going with Raquel?"

"En'. He told me a little while ago," Niigaanii chuckles, "That boy's excited." He puts his hands on her waist and pulls her close. The look in his eyes, asking what she wants, if she wants him.

He decides to play his final card. He gives her the double blueberry.

She leans into him, pushing against his kickstand. She feeds the berry to him before going in for a taste, "Bibs is never gonna sign your purchase order," she says.

"Huh?"

"Because I'm never leaving."

He grins, "Told you we have the best blueberries in Rainy Bay."

The sound of smacking lips other than their own breaks off their kiss.

"Mr. Puppers!" Niigaanii says.

The dog laps at ogaa naboob left on the bench of a picnic table nearby.

"Winnow made that," he tells the dog, "What do you think?"

Mr. Puppers cleans the bowl and gives a quiet *woof!* before trotting off.

"He likes it!" Niigaanii says and laughs.

"That's your friend with one and a half ears?"

He grins and then quickly leans around her, "Is that...Chris?"

Chris runs across the parking lot and gets into his car.

"That's the perv who tried to get into my room!" The MMA fighter yells, chasing after him.

As Chris' car speeds out of view, Winnow says, "What a moo jiid."

Bruce appears, his pants splattered with paint, "Sup, cuz?" he says to Niigaanii.

"Winnow, this is my cousin, Bruce the Little Moose."

"Boozhoo," she says.

Bruce flashes Winnow a perfect, white toothy smile, "You can call me Moozoons."

"Don't get wooed by that fancy glare of his, Moozoons here jumped from the back of the bleachers when we were fifteen and got himself a new set of chompers."

Bruce's mouth drops open. He looks from Niigaanii to Winnow and nods his head approvingly, "Alright, cuz, I gotta run, I got a mural to paint in Saint Paul. You two enjoy yourselves."

Winnow

After a walk through the festival, Winnow and Niigaanii stand in line for a wild berry snow cone.

Natalie, the girl who lost her shoe earlier in the week, approaches Winnow and holds out a corn husk doll, "I made this for you," she says.

"What? You made this for me?" Winnow gasps, "She's beautiful, thank you!"

The little doll has multicolored strands of corn husk hair, a husk dress, and tiny shoes that look like Natalie's jellies.

"These are my favorite shoes," Natalie says, pointing to the doll's feet. She smiles and runs off.

Bibs walks over carrying two plates of food. Her stride is sturdier than earlier in the week.

"You two eat yet?" she asks them.

"Not yet," Niigaanii says.

"Giwiisin," Bibs says and offers Winnow a plate.

"Chi-miigwech," Winnow says and starts cramming food in her mouth.

Niigaanii does the same.

Bibs pulls a handful of napkins from her back pocket and holds them up.

"I'm ok, thanks," Winnow says, wiping a dirty paw across her jeans.

Niigaanii waves his hand "no" and then uses the back of it to corral food off his cheek.

Bibs chuckles and makes her way.

"I told you I found you a wife," Merle says, adding his plate to a compost bin nearby.

"Boozhoo," Winnow says, blushing.

"I hope everyone here is making you feel at home," Merle says.

She looks at Niigaanii, "They sure are."

"How did you two meet?" Niigaanii says.

"I was cooking at a food summit last winter, and Merle and his wife were selling some delicious teas like the one you drank up on me the other day."

Niigaanii laughs, "But you didn't even know her name," he says to Merle.

Merle shrugs, "I lost my address book." He taps the new one in pocket of his button-up.

Niigaanii chuckles, "I guess I owe you a thank you then, Merle."

"Nothing says thank you like a nice big bucket of blueberries."

Niigaanii turns to Winnow with a dopey smile all for her, "You wanna go pick blueberries for Merle? And, uh, maybe go back to that mossy overlook we found on the island?"

"The one with the view of the lake and little cedar trees around that smell amazing?"

"That's the one."

Delores whizzes by and flaps him on the arm, "Go on den, get outta here you horny old thing."

Niigaanii drops his head back in a belly laugh.

Resisting the urge to tug on parts unseen, Winnow pulls on his hands, "Sko skettit."

On their walk to The Harvester, they run into Melanie.

"You tell that gaper, Chris, to beat it?" Melanie says, "I saw him running with his tail between his legs in the parking lot."

"Jeez, who didn't?" Winnow says and gives Melanie a big hug, "How's your auntie?'

"She's better, thanks."

"You must be Melanie," Niigaanii says, chuckling.

"Winnow!" The MMA fighter says, walking towards the festival, "Thanks for letting me crash in your room and for introducing me to Pete. We've been hitting it off if you know what I mean." She winks and continues on her way.

"Who's Pete?" Niigaanii asks.

"Yeah, who's Pete and why didn't you introduce him to me?" Melanie chimes in.

Winnow shakes her head, "I don't know. Pete?" and then she remembers Melanie's present was on the spare bed the day she left for the island, the same day she let the MMA fighter bunk in her room. She was so busy, she forgot all about it.

"Ooh!" Winnow throws her hands up to cover the loudest laugh her adult body has ever produced.

***

A few weeks later...

Winnow hands Melanie a jar of dried sumac fruit from a box labeled "kitchen stuff".

Melanie finds an empty spot for it on a shelf amongst the jars of herbs in Niigaanii's cabin.

"What's that?" Melanie says, motioning to an oblong gift box on the floor.

"New bathroom decor," Winnow says and fetches the box. She holds it open for Melanie to see the inscription burned into the wood with a fancy script.

"Don't forget to wash your ass," Melanie reads aloud. When she's stopped laughing, she says, "You know, it's BS I haven't seen Little Moose yet."

"Niigaanii said he's painting a mural in New Mexico at some big art fair down there. You'll have to wait for him to come back... or go chase after him."

"An art fair in New Mexico, huh? Maybe I *will* go."

Dear Reader,

If you loved this book, please leave me a review wherever you discover, buy, and read books; and don't forget to tell all of your friends!

www.realnativeromance.com

About the Author

Tashia Hart is an author, illustrator, and artist from the Red Lake Nation of Anishinaabeg. Her works include *Native Love Jams* (Not Too Far Removed Press, 2023), *The Goodberry Cookbook* (Minnesota Historical Society Press, 2021), *Gidjie and the Wolves* (Not Too Far Removed Press, 2020), and *Girl Unreserved* (2015). She's the illustrator of 3 children's books in the Minnesota Native American Lives series (Wise Ink Creative Publishing, 2020), and her short works include recipes, essays, poetry, and short stories for various publications. Tashia has worked in Indigenous kitchens and gardens, led foraging walks, and has a biology degree from Bemidji State University. She lives in Duluth, MN with her husband, son, and a turtle.

Visit www.tashiahart.com for more information.

41627178R00090